YOU HAVE REAC

Daughter contradicts mother. Niec
The spare, elegant stories in Louise Marburg's new book feature characters struggling to define themselves in a world that keeps confounding and contradicting them. Long-cherished ideas are examined and sometimes shattered, and lives are reshaped before our eyes. In Marburg's world, relationships are always subject to radical change, and her characters' destinations are unexpected, remarkable, and beautifully memorable.

~ ERIN MCGRAW, author of Joy and 52 Other Very Short Stories

The best short stories soar because of their author's wisdom, their knowledge of human nature, their ability to telegraph that knowledge in this odd, compressed form. Louise Marburg has that rare wisdom; her fiction absolutely hums with it, and yes, soars. This book is enlightening, challenging, and moving. I am so glad it is out in the world.

~ROBIN BLACK, author of Life Drawing and If I Loved You, I Would Tell You This

In her new collection, You Have Reached Your Destination, Louise Marburg has assembled a cast of badly behaved women I couldn't help but adore. Hilarious, irreverent, and tender hearted, her characters inspire empathy for them and compassion for ourselves. Warning: May cause addiction to Marburg's writing and sudden cravings for her other collections.

~R.L. MAIZES, author of Other People's Pets, winner of the Colorado Book Award, and We Love Anderson Cooper

An artful collection of stories, with vibes of Edward Hopper's New York. Exquisitely lonely, fraught with the ache of last chances, yet rendered with hope and love and humor, these stories left my heart lurching: What just flattened me? How did she do that?

~LESLIE PIETRZYK, author of Admit This to No One

You Have Reached Your Destination is a striking collection of short stories about the desires and destinations that too often elude us. What never fails, never eludes, is Marburg's affecting depiction of the strange, painful and wondrous.

~ ETHEL ROHAN, author of In the Event of Contact

You Have Reached Your Destination is a brilliantly subtle and elegantly crafted collection about fractured families, primal wounds, and lost opportunities, resilience, forgiveness, and the vibrancy of solitary lives. I greatly admired Louise Marburg's portrayal of women taking care of children, parents, friends, and neighbors while taking stock of their own experiences, women on the verge of regarding themselves with new excitement and tenderness.

~MARY SOUTH, author of You Will Never be Forgotten

YOU HAVE REACHED YOUR DESTINATION

STORIES

Louise Marburg

You Have Reached Your Destination
Louise Marburg

ISBN   978-1-958094-00-6

FICTION

BOOK DESIGN by EK Larken
COVER DESIGN by Lauren Crawford

Grateful acknowledgment is made to the publications in which the following stories appear:
"Alouette" in *STORY*; "The One That Scares You Most" in *Cimarron Review*; "Love Is Not Enough" in *The Hudson Review*; "The Weather of Menopause" in *Los Angeles Review*; "Even-Steven" in *Narrative*; "Vivian Delmar" in *Joyland*; "You Have Reached Your Destination" in a different form in *The Hudson Review*; "Outrageous" in *Atticus Review*; "Double Happiness" in *Post Road*; "Dance Rockette" in *Cutleaf*; "Next of Kin" in *The Hudson Review*.

PUBLISHED IN THE UNITED STATES OF AMERICA BY

EASTOVER
— PRESS —

Rochester, Massachusetts
www.EastOverPress.com

FOR CHARLIE, AGAIN AND ALWAYS

CONTENTS

ALOUETTE

When Penelope's fertility doctor mentioned her age twice in the same sentence—"Certainly it's not impossible for a thirty-seven-year-old to conceive for the first time, though thirty-seven is on the downslope of fertility"—she shook her head and gave him the same pitying look she gave her students when they were being stupid.

"I'm thirty-two," she said. The doctor opened the manila folder that held the form she'd filled out in the waiting room.

"It says thirty-seven here," he said.

"It does?" She leaned forward and looked. "Oh, no, that's meant to be a two, not a seven. My handwriting is a mess." She took a pen from her purse and added a tail to the seven. "There," she said. "Thirty-two." Her birth date was also written on the form, but the doctor didn't notice that. He closed the folder and smiled. She'd become a different person in his eyes, a patient with a promising outcome. He was pale and chubby and very young; his voice was high and oddly compressed, as if he'd taken a hit off a helium balloon. But judging by the layers of baby pictures and thank you cards pinned on a corkboard in the waiting room, he knew what he was doing. A fake orchid sat on his fake wood desk, and framed pictures of his three children were lined up on a shelf in a glass and chrome bookcase behind him.

"Why do you put your photos where you can't see them?"

she said.

He swiveled his chair. "I can if I turn around."

"Have you considered the effect that has on your patients, being forced to look at the examples of your obviously robust fertility when it's quite possible they might not be fertile themselves?"

A little frown creased his forehead. "No, I hadn't."

"Well, you should." She sniffed and took a tissue from a box on his desk. "Don't worry, I'm not going to cry. I have allergies this time of year." She blew her nose. "So," she said brightly. "What's next?"

Russ showed up while she was having her blood drawn. He looked important in his dark business suit. "I was held up at work," he said, inching around a Formica counter.

"Did they catch the guy?" Penelope said.

"What guy?"

"The guy who held you up."

The nurse drawing her blood chuckled. "Good one."

"Russ, this is Rhoda," Penelope said. "She says I have to give her permission to test my blood for HIV. Should I?"

"You just said you have to, so yes," Russ said.

"But what if I have it?"

"You don't have it."

"I might, you never know." She gave Rhoda a wide-eyed look.

"You're quite the card," Rhoda said. "How long have you two been married?"

"Long," Penelope said. "We're well past the incubation period, unless my husband has something to tell me."

Rhoda gathered up her equipment. "We're done here. You can go."

Penelope rolled down her sleeve and slid off the table. There was no way she had HIV, yet she was capable of convincing herself of anything. A few years ago, she was sure she saw President Obama coming out of Lahore, a Pakistani restaurant down the street from her apartment. She swore to Russ that she'd seen the President, insisted she had to her friends, until finally she was forced to accept the fact that the President of the United States wouldn't go anywhere alone, never mind to Lahore, which wasn't even that good.

They left the doctor's office and went to lunch at a place by Central Park that served grilled sandwiches and a variety of milkshakes. They sat at a table outside. Penelope pretended she was already pregnant and ordered a strawberry-banana shake that probably contained an entire day's worth of calories. The trees in the park were tossing; the sky was an unblemished blue. The perfection of the day was a good omen. She fiddled with the carnelian bead she wore on a silver chain around her neck. She'd bought the bead at a New Age shop in the Village because carnelians promoted fertility.

She took a long draw on her milkshake and sighed with satisfaction. "Just think, this time next year we could be parents."

"Don't count your chickens," Russ said.

"I'm not. They're also testing my blood for chlamydia. I won't be able to have a baby if I've had chlamydia: it wrecks your reproductive system. By the way, if anyone asks, I'm thirty-two."

"Why are you thirty-two?"

"Can I pass for thirty-two?"

"Why not." His eyes were sometimes green and sometimes blue, and his hair was a rich shade of auburn. Penelope hoped their child would take after him. She was attractive enough, but nothing special. "You're not going to start obsessing about chlamydia I hope."

She bit into her sandwich, a gooey four-cheese production. She would be the fattest pregnant woman ever. "You can have chlamydia and not even know it. Hepatitis C is called the silent killer; they're testing my blood for that too." She gave Russ the same goggle-eyed look she'd given

Rhoda. "I could be dying right now."

He mimicked her expression, teasing her. "We're all dying right now."

For years Penelope hadn't wanted a child. She taught French at a private elementary school on the Upper East Side and knew what children were like. "I already have ninety of them," she would say. "That's more than enough for me." Russ didn't care about children one way or the other, and neither did his parents, who in any case lived in Hawaii. Penelope's brisk, cheerful mother—a speed walker, a book grouper—had been fatally hit by a city bus when Penelope was twenty-four; her father remarried a woman with two young sons, then they together had twins, unplanned. "Fertile Myrtle," Penelope called her stepmother behind her back. She called her father "The Old Goat." Then one day she was leading the pre-K class in a dissonant round of "Alouette" when she had a gut-punching vision of herself singing "Alouette" to her own child, a toothlessly smiling baby girl. She'd been thirty-five at the time, which didn't seem too old, but two years of trying had produced nothing more than a bunch of negative pregnancy tests.

"You should have started this earlier," Russ had said.

"We," she'd said. "We should have started earlier. You didn't want a baby either. If you'd wanted one, I would have wanted one too." She missed her mother, who would have pushed for grandchildren, and hated her father for his inattention. She resented Russ's unencouraging attitude. She would have liked someone to give a damn.

A week after her blood was drawn, she went back to the doctor. She sat on a hard chair in the crowded waiting room for more than an hour, steeling herself for being told she had HIV, or chlamydia, or hepatitis C, or a combination of all three. Surreptitiously, she assessed the other patients. Most of them seemed too young to be infertile, but there was one who looked too old to even be trying, judging by the brittle skin around her eyes. Someone's husband read a magazine; another played a game on his phone. Both seemed oblivious to the buzzing anxiety that filled the room like an expanding balloon. Penelope got up and went to the reception desk.

"How much longer?" she asked. The nurse shrugged and reached to catch a document that was being regurgitated from a fax machine.

"Not long," she said, which was what she'd said the last time. Penelope sat back down.

"I'm about to jump out of my skin," she said to the woman next to her. The woman was heavier than Penelope by many pounds. Penelope had read somewhere that fat contained estrogen.

"What stage are you at?" the woman said.

"Stage?" Penelope said.

"You know, where are you in the process?"

"Oh. The beginning. What about you?"

"I'm on my fourth IVF," the woman said. "Fifty thousand dollars and I've got bubkes. If this one doesn't take, I don't know what we'll do."

Penelope stared at the woman. She hadn't thought as far as having to do this multiple times. They could barely afford to do it once. "Shit!" she said. So much for the fat-estrogen connection.

"Shit is right," the woman said. She reached into a canvas tote and took out some fine yellow knitting. "It's a baby blanket," she said. It was knit in delicate cables. "I started it a year and a half ago."

"Beautiful," Penelope said.

"Or tragic," the woman said.

Finally, Penelope's name was called. She followed a nurse to the doctor's office. He had removed his family pictures from the bookshelf and arranged them on his desk so they faced only him.

"Good idea," Penelope said, indicating the new arrangement, but when he looked at her quizzically, she realized he'd forgotten who she was. Her folder was open on his desk, containing what she assumed were the results of her blood test.

"I wish I had better news," he said.

Penelope froze. "What?"

"Your ovarian reserve is low. I don't like to see that in a woman your age. Undoubtedly that's why you haven't conceived. But it's not an insurmountable problem. We can proceed."

"That's great."

"We'll start you on a round of injections and harvest the eggs when they mature," he said. "In your case, I'm hoping for six or seven viable eggs. Optimally, we like to see ten to twenty, but..." He gave her a clownish frown.

"Harvest? As in reap?"

"Exactly." He closed the folder.

"That's like something out of a misogynistic sci-fi movie, harvest the eggs." She shivered.

"How else would you put it?"

"Extract, maybe? I don't know."

"Well." He stood and offered his small, fat hand. He'd never shaken her hand before, and she wondered about this sudden civility.

"Am I not going to see you again?"

"Of course you are, when I harvest your eggs. Right now you'll see Rhoda. She'll set you up with your injections."

Rhoda did remember Penelope, which Penelope found very cheering. They sat in an office whose single window looked out onto a tree that threw moving shadows across the bare walls.

"Pretty," Penelope said of the shadows.

"Thank you," Rhoda said. "It used to be shoulder-length,

but I needed a change." She touched the back of her shining dark hair, which was boy-short and styled into rigid waves across the crown of her head. "I broke up with my fiancé last month. We were engaged six years and I was, like, it's time to shit or get off the pot."

"They say you shouldn't do anything drastic to your appearance after a breakup."

"I've heard that too." Rhoda picked up a syringe that lay on the desk between them. "Okay, here we go. You got your syringe; you got your medication." She tapped a small vial of powder with one long glittering fingernail, then picked up a second vial filled with liquid. "This is your diluent. Carefully, you take the cap off your syringe. Do not touch the needle." She inserted the needle into the rubber top of the vial of liquid. "Draw up exactly 1 cc of the diluent. You can see how much 1 cc is because it's marked on the side of the syringe."

Penelope leaned in and examined the syringe. "Got it."

"Then you take your syringe and insert the needle into the vial of medication. Slowly inject the solution into the powder. See? Like I'm doing now. Don't inject it too fast, and do not shake the vial."

"I won't," Penelope said.

"When the medication is diluted, draw up exactly 1 cc of the liquid, raise your syringe, and tap out any air bubbles there might be." She flicked the side of the syringe. Her hands were long and graceful. "It's important you do this just like I'm showing you. Then, when you're sure you got everything right, inject the medication into your butt."

"I don't know if I can reach back there with a syringe."

"Not you, honey, your husband. And don't forget to sterilize the injection site with alcohol. This is a hormone you'll be taking, so it might make you feel a little nutty." She took a couple of boxes of vials and a plastic bag full of syringes out of a desk drawer and pushed the equipment across the desk to Penelope like a raft to the opposite shore.

The woman at the New Age shop who'd sold Penelope her carnelian fertility bead had recommended a psychic named Clair Voyant.

"Clair Voyant isn't her real name, obviously," the woman had said as she handed Penelope Clair's card. "But that's the only thing that's phony about her. She's brilliant with the tarot cards. I have a lot of customers who swear by her."

"Oh, I don't know," Penelope had said. "What if she says I won't get pregnant?"

"That's the chance you take, but wouldn't you rather be prepared?"

"No," Penelope said.

But after starting the injections, she felt a surge of optimism. She told Russ she'd made an appointment with Clair Voyant.

"She's supposed to be amazing," she said.

"An amazing rip-off," Russ said. He popped the top off a bottle of beer. "You're not into that woo-woo shit."

"I am too." She grabbed the beer from him and took a long swig. Knowing she wouldn't be allowed to drink alcohol while she was pregnant made her want to drink as much as possible now. She opened a cupboard below the kitchen counter and took out a bottle of gin.

"Then why haven't you ever talked about it before?"

"Just because I've never talked about something with you doesn't mean I don't believe in it."

"Name one other weird thing you believe in that you haven't told me about."

She thought a minute. "The Bermuda Triangle," she finally said for lack of a better answer.

Clair Voyant lived in a part of Brooklyn that required a change of trains; when Penelope emerged from the subway, she felt like she'd traveled to another country. There weren't any shops or restaurants or apartments, only vast concrete buildings and a factory of some kind that leaked a mirage-like vapor from a series of gray chimney stacks. Following the directions on her phone, she made her way through empty side streets to a two-story brick house that was squeezed between a reeking car repair shop and an industrial appliance wholesaler. Clair opened the door before Penelope could knock. She was an elfin young woman who wore a plain white T-shirt and a pair of khaki shorts.

"You don't look the way I thought you would," Penelope said.

"I get that a lot," Clair said. "But nobody can say what they expected me to look like."

"I can't really either," Penelope said. "Less normal, I guess."

"Whatever normal looks like," Clair said.

She led Penelope down a hall to a little room where an overhead fixture cast a weak yellow light. She indicated that Penelope should sit in a ratty armchair, its stuffing bulging from holes in the fake leather upholstery. Across from it was a less ratty armchair, and between them, a round brass-topped table. An ornate, gilded painting of a winged figure was the only picture hanging on the dingy white walls.

"I dreamt about you last night," Clair said. "I saw you with a group of children. It looked like you were at a playground."

Penelope gasped. "I'm a grade school teacher!"

"Ah, that explains it," Clair said. She sat down and picked up a pack of cards off the table. She shuffled the cards and placed them before Penelope. "My dreams are usually prophetic, but sometimes they're just factual." She smiled, revealing a wide gap between her front teeth. She had a nearly unnoticeable lisp, a tiny whistle, that must have been because of the gap. "Shuffle three times and then cut the deck into three piles."

Penelope did as she was told. The cards were larger than playing cards and awkward to shuffle. She cut the deck. Clair gathered up the cards and lay down ten of them in a circle on the brass table. She studied them.

"I can see you're on the threshold of something new," she said.

"Yes, I am," Penelope said. "Or I hope I am."

"This thing is important to you."

"It really is. Should I tell you? Is that okay?"

"Sure." *Thsure.*

"I'm trying to have a baby."

Clair picked up a card that had a single cup on it. "Oh yes. I can see her. She's beautiful."

"Her?"

"Yes, you're going to have a girl. I'm so glad for you."

"Can you tell me when?"

Clair closed her eyes and pressed her temple with two fingers. "I see sunshine and green grass."

"Maybe May?"

"Yes, May."

"Oh, thank God." Penelope felt almost nauseated with relief.

"You're a magical person, Penelope. Have you been told that before?"

"No, I haven't. I don't think of myself that way. My life is kind of ho-hum, actually."

"That will change," Clair said. "Magical things happen to magical people."

"What kind of magical things can I expect?"

"Just wait, you'll see," Clair said. "Your vibration is very strong." She picked up another card. "I'm sensing a darkness from the other side." She showed Penelope the card, which did indeed look forbidding. A gargoyle-like figure and a man and a woman were bound to each other by chains. "The

Devil speaks of a jealous spirit who seeks to thwart you. Sometimes a dark spirit from the other side attaches to an individual on this side. It's nobody you know, just a roving, restless spirit. You need to send it away so your pregnancy will be healthy."

Penelope felt a chair spring spear the back of her thigh as she sat forward. She didn't know what "the other side" was, but if it contained dark spirits she was happy to remain ignorant of it. "How do I do that?"

Clair got up, left the room, and came back with a glass cylinder that held a blue candle. "Burn this candle for an hour every evening. It's imbued with positive energy. I can give it to you for seventy-five."

Penelope looked at the candle. It was similar to a candle she'd seen in Crate and Barrel, yet totally different somehow. She felt the dark spirit as a shadow behind her, breathing down her neck. That she would attract such malevolence shocked her. "Will you take a check?" she said, digging into her purse. "I'm not sure I have that much . . ."

"Plus a hundred for the reading," Clair said. "Make it out to cash."

On the train back to Manhattan, Penelope wished she'd asked Clair Voyant her real name. Would Clair have told her? Penelope thought so. The personal nature of their conversation had made Penelope feel like they were friends; they'd hugged each other in parting, Penelope tearily grateful. As the train rattled across Brooklyn, she felt exhilarated and impatient. Lost in thought or listening to music, the other passengers were unaware of her radiance. The woman next to her was doing the *Times* crossword. She was about the age Penelope's mother would have been. Penelope looked over her shoulder until the woman turned and asked, "Are you a crossword lover, too?"

"Sorry," Penelope said. "I couldn't help looking."

"A six-letter word for a 'chilly baked treat,'" the woman

said.

"Pardon me?" Penelope had never done a crossword puzzle.

"That's the clue."

"Oh. Gosh, I don't know. My head has been in the clouds since I got pregnant." She patted her belly. "The little scoundrel is stealing my brain cells."

"Pregnant! Wonderful!" the woman said. She seemed genuinely pleased. "How far along?"

"Twelve weeks. I'm so excited."

"Your first?"

"Yes. It's a girl. I found out today."

"Oh, a girl," the woman said. "I have a daughter. Have you thought of any names?"

"Etienne," Penelope said.

"That's unusual."

"It's French. I'm French. My daughter is going to be bilingual."

"What a lucky, lucky girl."

"She really will be." Penelope looked out the smeary car window as the train came into a station. She wasn't a liar, or not much of one, normally. Not this much of a liar. Who knew what else would come out of her mouth if she didn't stop talking: she was starting to believe herself.

The egg-harvesting procedure was supposed to be painful, so Penelope would be sedated with the same drug that killed Michael Jackson.

"It's called propofol," the doctor said as the anesthesiologist rigged her up. "It's perfectly safe if you don't abuse it. When you wake up, you'll feel like you weren't even out."

Penelope was lying flat with her feet up in stirrups. She raised her head. "I'll be completely out?"

"Of course," the doctor said.

"How will I know what you're doing, then? I mean, you could be doing anything to me."

"Don't worry," Rhoda said with a wink. "I'll keep an eye on him."

"Oh for God's sake," the doctor said. "Go to sleep."

When Penelope woke, the doctor was gone, and Russ was sitting beside her in a plastic chair, his chin on his chest, asleep. His tie had been loosened and his shirt collar was open; his suit jacket hung on the back of the chair. She looked at him fondly. Dutifully, he'd injected her with the hormones that had made her feel as nutty as Rhoda had predicted; she'd snapped at him so often she'd begun to dislike herself. They'd ridden the waves of marriage for almost thirteen years. Seven years ago, she became infatuated for several months with a fellow teacher, a younger man who had an apartment near school where they would fuck while Russ was at work. Russ must have sensed something different about her even if he hadn't known what—or maybe he had known and hadn't wanted to let on, hoping it would blow over. Ever since then, she'd been waiting for some kind of karmic retribution. Maybe her infertility was it.

He woke slowly and looked at her as if she'd appeared from thin air. "You're supposed to lie here a while," he said.

"You hate change, don't you?" she said. "Chaos is your worst nightmare. That's why you never wanted a baby, isn't it, because it would completely upend your life."

"I like my life the way it is, I admit it," he said. "I like you the way you are. I don't need anything else."

"Do you know why I want a baby?"

"Tell me."

"Because I want someone in my life who can't not love me."

"I love you."

"But you can fall out of love with me, and there was a time when you didn't love me, before you knew me. My baby will never not have known me, will never not have loved me. She'll love me forever. And no one will love her more than I do. That was how I felt with my mother, that no one in the world would love me as much as she did."

"You think it'll be a girl?"

"That's what Clair told me."

"Is that so?"

"I want someone to miss me the way I miss my mom."

"I would miss you if you died."

"Hah, right," she said. "My mother wasn't dead two years before my father remarried."

Russ took her hand. "Sweetheart, what if this doesn't work?"

Penelope frowned. "It'll work. Clair told me it would."

"Clair is a scammer," he said gently. "Psychics or readers, whatever you want to call them, they don't really know anything. They're in it for the money. That candle she sold you? It's just a candle. She's a scam artist."

Penelope had been lighting the candle faithfully, refusing to tempt fate with doubt. "She isn't like that, Russ. She said she dreamt about me surrounded by kids on a playground, she saw I'm a teacher even before we met!"

"She Googled you. Anyone can find out you're a teacher." He took out his phone and tapped in Penelope's name. "See?" He turned the phone so she could see it. "There you are on the school's website." It was a headshot, identifying her as a French teacher.

Penelope gazed at the photo of her face. "She said I'd give birth in May."

"Did she tell you that, or did you tell her that's what you want?"

Penelope sat up and tore away the paper sheet that covered her. "It's going to work." She got off the table and put on her pants. She sat back down. "What if it doesn't?"

"Then it doesn't," Russ said.

"You don't care, do you?"

He raked his hand through his beautiful hair. "I care about you."

"Never mind," she said and left the room.

Rhoda passed her in the hall carrying an armful of manila file folders. "I'll call you tomorrow and let you know how many embryos are viable," she said. "We'll transfer them on Thursday."

"What are my chances?" Penelope said.

Rhoda stopped. "Around twenty-five percent."

Penelope gaped at her. "Are you shitting me? That's all?"

"Think positive," Rhoda said. "Try not to work yourself up."

Penelope walked out into the waiting room. It was crowded as usual, the atmosphere dense with anticipation. The woman with the baby blanket was back again, as well as the husband playing a game on his phone. The nurse behind the desk beckoned with Penelope's bill in hand. There was nothing magical about it.

THE ONE THAT SCARES YOU MOST

Lisa was forty-one when her mother had a stroke. Her brother Teddy called to tell her about it. It had been twenty-three years since she had spoken to her mother and a few weeks since she'd talked to Teddy, who worked as a life coach. The thought that anyone would pay Teddy for his advice made Lisa laugh. He was morbidly obese, a diabetic who smoked. The life coaching thing was new.

"She woke up a different person," Teddy said about their mother. "She's nice now."

"What do you mean, *nice?*" Lisa said.

"Nice like sweet," he said. "She's been asking for you. And for Dad. She'd forgotten they're divorced. When I told her, she cried. It was weird. I don't think I've ever seen her cry before, have you?"

"She doesn't cry, she makes people cry. She made you cry all the time."

"I've forgiven her," Teddy said piously. *Of course you have,* Lisa thought. Most of Teddy's income was doled out to him by their mother; she'd been floating him for decades. When she died, Teddy would be wealthy. He was counting on it.

"When did this happen?"

"This morning. I wanted to call you earlier."

"Why?" Lisa said.

"Because I thought you should know." He was trying to

sound grave, but she could hear a thread of anxiety in his voice.

"Is she still a drunk?"

Teddy sighed. "She hasn't asked for a drink, if that's what you mean. She hasn't been drinking as heavily as she used to the past few years. I wouldn't call her a drunk."

"You never did," Lisa said.

Opening a kitchen cupboard, she took out a box of graham crackers, then went to the refrigerator for lemonade. Her five-year-old daughter Rosie had a friend over; they would be wanting a snack any minute. She looked through the French doors that led out to the back patio. Rosie and her friend Bella were sitting on an iron loveseat grooming their American Girl dolls. The day was hot, and Rosie's face was as flushed as a peach. Lisa's husband, Peter, was on his knees, weeding the lush bed of hosta at the foot of the tall wooden fence between their brownstone and the neighbor's. Peter thought Teddy was an idiot. He'd never met Lisa's mother.

"She's going home tomorrow," Teddy said. "I called a service the hospital recommended; they're sending a nurse. She's weak on her left side. I guess you should wait until Monday to see her."

"See her?" Lisa said. She poured the lemonade into two glasses. "What makes you think I want to see her? This is your problem, Teddy. She's all yours."

"I need you," Teddy said.

"What for? You said you hired a nurse."

"The doctor said it's likely she'll have another stroke. She could be paralyzed next time; she might lose her speech. She could die!"

"Isn't that what you've been waiting for all these years?"

"What? Don't say that!"

"Okay, well, let me know when she does die. Actually, no, don't."

"But she's asked to see you," he said.

"Don't care," she said.

"How can you be so unfeeling?"

"Easily," she said and hung up. She set out the lemonade and crackers and called Rosie and Bella inside.

"Can we have Oreos?" Rosie said.

"Graham crackers are healthier than Oreos," Lisa said. She wrapped her arms loosely around her daughter's neck and breathed in Rosie's hair. It was warm and smelled of strawberry shampoo, blond like Peter's, thick and curly. It was a piece of luck, having such a delicious child. She would have stayed like that for the rest of the afternoon if Rosie hadn't wriggled in protest.

"Mommy, no," she said, aggrieved. Reluctantly, Lisa let her go and went outside to talk to Peter.

"Hello there," he said cheerily as she came up behind him. "Come to help me, I hope?"

"Suzanne had a stroke," she said. She hadn't referred to her mother as "Mom" since the day Suzanne prevented her from entering the apartment where she'd grown up by changing the lock on the door. Lisa had been seventeen, a senior in high school. She'd had to go live with her father in New Jersey and switch schools in the middle of the year. "Teddy called. Apparently Suzanne has amnesia and has forgotten what a bitch she is."

Peter sat on his heels and brushed soil from his hands. "Seriously?"

"That's what he says."

She knelt beside him and violently pulled a dandelion out of the ground by its roots. "He says the stroke has made her nice. How can a person who's never had a kind moment in her life suddenly become nice? I don't see how a stroke could do that."

"Strokes can affect any part of the brain. A personality change isn't uncommon," Peter said. He was the kind of person who read everything and had all sorts of facts at hand.

Lisa never doubted anything he said. She depended on him being right the way other women depended on their husbands being handy around the house.

"There isn't a molecule in Suzanne's brain that contains nice," she said.

"What does it matter what she's like now?"

"She doesn't get to be a nasty drunk for her whole adult life and then go out as a sober sweetheart. She doesn't get to forget who she was."

"Why don't you tell her who she was, then? Now's your opportunity."

"Because she asked for me to go see her, and I refuse to give her what she wants. Yes, I am that small."

"You're that angry," Peter said.

She pinched a weed and yanked. "Yep. Small and angry."

When Lisa went to live with her father, he'd been at the end of his second marriage. Her stepmother wasn't a terrible person, but she'd fallen in love with another man and was on her way out the door. "Good," she'd said when Lisa showed up. "You can keep him company. You're peas in a pod, you'll have a grand time together."

It was true that they were alike. Lisa had inherited her father's prominent nose and straight black hair, his love of words and facts. If their time hadn't been exactly grand, it hadn't been unpleasant: her father had swayed admirably in the emotional weather of a displaced teenaged girl. Though at the time Lisa felt herself to be deeply unhappy, she looked back on their months together fondly, the creatively concocted meals and invigorating yardwork, their shared enthusiasm for Scrabble. She'd never before had her father to herself for any length of time. They became close by dint of maneuvering around each other, finding points of connection here and there like small gifts laid at their door. She had been seven when her parents divorced. She could not imagine being divorced from Peter. There was nothing about her parents' lives that she could imagine for herself.

A few days after Teddy's news, Lisa met her father at a midtown restaurant for lunch. He rarely came into the city since he retired a few years ago, but he wanted to see her in person, he'd said, to talk about Suzanne. Teddy, the big baby, had called him.

"Honestly, I don't see what it has to do with you," Lisa said as they were being served their meals. "You were married to your second wife almost as long as you were to Suzanne, and you don't even know where Hilda is now."

"Hilda and I didn't have children together," he said. "Don't be mad at Teddy: he's in over his head."

"He's always in over his head," she said. "He just stumbles along doing whatever. Have you seen him recently? He's a whale."

Her father repositioned his water goblet on the tablecloth and made a sound in his throat. The restaurant was fancy, Italian. He always took her to expensive places and paid the check, which made her feel cherished and safe. He looked fresh in a pressed blue dress shirt and a blazer made of straw-colored linen. "Teddy isn't you, Lisa," he said.

"No kidding," she said.

"But he has some very good qualities."

"Such as?"

"Empathy."

"I'm plenty empathetic," Lisa said. She put down her fork. "Wait a minute. You think I should visit Suzanne, don't you? Wow, I'm surprised."

"Why? I've always wanted you to patch it up with your mother."

"She locked me out of the house."

"Well, you called her a drunk."

"No, I called her an alcoholic."

"The clinical term! That's even worse," her father said, and they laughed. "You know she would have taken you back if you'd apologized."

"I wasn't going to apologize for telling the truth," she said. "How many times do we have to go over this ground? You know what she was like, Dad. I'm glad I got away."

"I wish you'd known her when she was young. She was sharp as a tack, and so funny—irresistible, really, everyone loved her."

"I find that so hard to believe," Lisa said. *Blah, blah, blah,* she thought. She'd heard it before. They had gotten to the restaurant early, but now it was crowded, the atmosphere loud with broken conversations and scraping chairs, the clatter of silverware and china. She wished they could talk about something else. Lately, Rosie refused to play soccer for some reason she wouldn't divulge. The three of them were going on a family vacation to Cape May in a couple of weeks. Lisa was considering doing some freelance editing in addition to her publishing job, with the idea of eventually making it a full-time thing so she could work from home. She toyed with her pasta, spearing a single rotini. She'd lost her appetite.

"I was thinking—" she began.

"Alcoholism is a disease," her father said.

"So I should give Suzanne a pass, is what you're saying. I should feel sorry for her. The poor woman was a victim of forces beyond her control."

"Lisa."

"Dad. I'm not going to feel sorry for her. You know who I feel sorry for? Me."

"You turned out all right," he said without looking at her. When he did look up, his eyes were rheumy and tired. He was getting old, she thought with a pang.

"No thanks to anyone but myself," she said. "I don't remember you being any help."

"What do you mean? I took you in!"

"Excuse me? Took me in?" she said. "I wasn't some urchin, I was your daughter!"

She left the table and went down a long hallway to a ladies' room nearly too small to turn around in. Sliding the bolt, she leaned against the door and allowed herself to seethe. Her father had left her and Teddy with Suzanne knowing full well what their lives would be like without him as a buffer and responsible adult. Either Suzanne found reasons to be livid and screaming, or she acted as if her children didn't exist. When Lisa was twelve, she went with Suzanne on a train to upstate New York to visit Suzanne's mother. Teddy hadn't been with them. For four hours, the train had chugged through lush summer landscapes, lakes and mountains and forests, but the only thing Lisa remembered about the trip was that Suzanne hadn't spoken to her once. She'd been hungover, so Lisa knew to make herself small. It was in the days when smoking was still allowed, and they'd sat in the smoking car. Suzanne had smoked cigarette after cigarette while gazing at the back of the seat before her, either deeply lost in thought or trying not to jar her head. Lisa had found the dining car by herself and bought a three-dollar tuna sandwich, and Suzanne got up to use the bathroom once, sliding wordlessly past Lisa's knees. Lisa had no recollection of her grandmother or the visit, only Suzanne's relentless silence and the fug of cigarette smoke.

Someone rattled the door. "Occupied!" Her voice echoed off the tiles. She reapplied her lipstick and returned to the table composed. Her father had ordered them both tartufo, her favorite dessert.

"I was seventeen years old," she said as she sat down. "Seventeen, Dad. She kicked me out and somehow I've always been blamed. Please tell me: how does that compute?"

"I'm not saying you were to blame," he said. "But you're not seventeen anymore."

She cracked the chocolate shell on her tartufo with her

spoon. The ice cream inside was vanilla. The day Suzanne locked her out of the apartment, she'd been puzzled that the key wouldn't turn. She'd jiggled it and tried again. When no one answered the doorbell, she'd banged on the door until a neighbor came out and told her to stop.

"I don't know about that, Dad. A part of me will always be that seventeen-year-old girl."

"Oh, come on now, don't be dramatic," her father said.

"It's true," she said mildly. She didn't expect to be understood.

"You only have one mother, sweetheart."

"Right. And my mother had only one daughter."

She looked beyond him at her reflection in a long mirror across the room. She wore a tailored dress made of lilac silk with a square neckline that framed her collarbones; her long hair was pulled back into a sleek braided twist, revealing a pair of delicate gold hoops in her ears. She had an interesting job, a husband she loved, a daughter she adored. *I escaped*, she thought. *I freed myself.* And yet she had also been discarded.

Rosie loved Teddy, and Teddy loved her, so Lisa wasn't entirely surprised to come home from work and find her brother sitting cross-legged on the carpet in Rosie's room playing with her collection of horses. Rosie was in possession of the biggest, most realistic-looking horse in the collection; Teddy held a glittery little pony that had once decorated a cake. Peter had let him in an hour earlier and gone back to his computer.

"Let's go on a trail ride," Rosie said.

"Okay, partner," Teddy said. He looked up as Lisa came in. "Mommy's home."

"Mommy, Uncle Teddy's here!" Rosie said.

"I can see that, baby," Lisa said. "Can I borrow him?" She beckoned to Teddy, who arduously stood and followed her downstairs.

"She's smart as a whip, isn't she?" he said. "I bet she gets As in school."

"They don't give grades in kindergarten, but yeah, she reads everything. She's like her dad." She took a baking dish of marinating chicken out of the refrigerator, then opened a box of lettuce and dumped it into a wooden bowl. "Speaking of dads, I saw ours today."

"He's going to visit Mom, you know."

"No, he's not. He only told you he would to placate you. What is it with you wanting everybody to visit Suzanne?"

"She could die, Lisa. Don't you want to make things right again before that happens?"

"Right again?" she said. "What 'things' were ever right in the first place?"

"Don't you love her?" he said.

Lisa put the dish of chicken in the oven. "Of course I don't love her. I can't believe you have to ask."

"I can't believe you just said that! I don't think it's true. What kind of person doesn't love their mother?" He pinched the flesh between his eyebrows as if she'd given him a headache; his face and neck were flushed. His shirttails were half-untucked and his jaw was darkened by a day's worth of beard. *You're a mess*, Lisa thought. Very few of her and Peter's friends had met Teddy, and that was on purpose. He'd done a year and a half at a third-rate college and lived in a studio apartment in a bleak postwar building at the farthest reach of the Upper West Side. She had a master's degree in comparative literature. Peter was an economist. Their brownstone in Park Slope had three bedrooms, one of which Peter used as an office.

"Sit," she said. "Calm down." He sat at a long trestle table that was half-covered with books and mail.

Peter came in and took a bottle of red wine from a rack on top of the fridge. Lisa sat down across from Teddy. "I don't see how you can love Suzanne after the way she treated you—treated us—growing up. Why? Because she gives you money?"

"No," he said, offended. "I just do. People love their mothers."

"Not always. Some people don't love their mothers. And some mothers don't love their children."

Rosie came down from upstairs. She went to Lisa and squeezed against her side. "Is that true, Mommy?"

Lisa stroked her hair. "Is what true, Rosie Bear?"

"That some moms don't love their children."

Peter handed Lisa a glass of wine and gave her a narrow look. "Not in this house it's not," he said to Rosie.

"Uncle Teddy said his mom is Mommy's mom, too," she said.

"Really?" Lisa said. She looked at Teddy. "When did he say that?"

"When we were playing," Rosie said.

"What else did he say?"

"He said you and me and Daddy are going to go see her."

"No, we're not," Lisa said.

"But I want to go!" Rosie said.

Peter squatted down so he was eye level with Rosie. "Hey, Rosie, do you want to play on my computer?" Playing on the big computer was a rare treat, reserved for emergency distraction. They only had one innocuous game, called Carnival, which Rosie would play hours if they let her. Peter took Rosie's hand and led her away. "Work this out," he said to Lisa before they left the room.

"You are the most manipulative person on Earth," Lisa said to Teddy.

"She's been asking about you constantly," Teddy said. "She wants to know where you are, why she hasn't seen you."

"Did you tell her why?"

"Tell her yourself!" he shouted.

Lisa was shocked. "Don't yell at me and don't tell me what to do."

"She always loved you more than me," he said.

"Oh for God's sake," she said. "How could you even tell? She acted like she hated us both. Anyway, obviously she loves you, or she wouldn't have supported you financially all these years."

Evening was falling, and the sun's last rays coming through the panes of the French doors created golden rectangles on the floor. The baking chicken smelled delicious. Lisa could hear Rosie's squealing laughter upstairs. She made a wide circular motion with her finger as if to encompass it all. "This is my life, Teddy. I made it all by myself."

"You think my life is crap," he said.

Lisa folded her hands on the table. "Truth? I think Suzanne screwed you up and made you not value yourself. I think that's why you don't take care of yourself and can't sustain a relationship or have a career. I think she crippled you, and she gives you money because she knows it and feels guilty."

Teddy stood and went out to the patio. Lisa watched him fish a pack of cigarettes out of the back pocket of his jeans and light up. He'd been smoking since he was thirteen, filching Suzanne's Marlboro Lights; he would doubtless die young. She got up and went out to him.

"Drag?" she said. He passed her the cigarette. A cricket shrieked from somewhere. The traffic on Ninth Street was faintly audible. She thought about the trip to Cape May. "I'm sorry if I hurt your feelings, but that's what I think. If you'd gotten away from her, you'd have had a happier life."

"She tells me she loves me all the time now," he said.

"Then what's all this about her loving me more?" She handed back the cigarette.

"She was meaner to me when we were growing up."

"That was only because you provoked her."

They stood in silence. She could hear his breathing and smell his odor, a combination of armpit and tobacco.

"How's the life coaching?" she said after a while.

"I couldn't get it off the ground," he said. "I'm thinking about getting a real estate license."

"Do you really think Suzanne will die soon?"

"I think she might have a fatal stroke, yeah."

"Then you won't have to worry about having a job anymore."

He shifted his weight and blew out a stream of smoke. "That's not why I love her."

"I know. Leave this alone, will you, Teddy?"

"Is that really what you want?"

She laughed and turned to go back inside. "You must be deaf," she said.

The oppressively muggy weather turned overnight into the kind of bright, crisp day that Lisa envisioned when she thought about summer, though days like that were relatively few during August in the city. She got out of the subway two stops early so her walk to work would be longer, bouncing along in a pair of sneakers she would exchange for proper shoes at the office. Her phone rang. She fished it out of her bag, looked at the unfamiliar number, and immediately dropped it back in. A few minutes later, it rang again, showing the same number. Thinking it might be someone from Rosie's day camp, she answered.

"There you are!" a cheerful voice said. "Are you coming to see me soon?"

Lisa ducked into the entryway of a building. Suzanne's voice was higher than she remembered. "How did you get this number?" She felt the harshness of her own voice in her throat.

"Teddy gave it to me," Suzanne said.

"I'm busy," Lisa said and hung up. She held her phone in a shaking hand as she punched in Teddy's number. "You fucking asshole," she said when he answered.

"What?" he said.

"Suzanne just called me. You gave her my number." Teddy didn't reply. "What the hell, Teddy? You agreed to stop this shit."

"I did, but that was after I gave her your number."

"You had no right."

"Change your number then."

"That's what I'll do," she said.

At work, she handed her phone to her assistant and asked her to take it to Verizon.

"You have to do that, they won't let me," Britney said. She was very young but far more confident than Lisa had been at her age. "Why do you want to change it? You're going to have to alert all your contacts, it'll be a big pain."

"I'm being harassed," Lisa said.

"No kidding," Britney said. "Do you know who it is?"

Lisa paused. She had yet to meet anyone who could comprehend her relationship with Suzanne. Britney talked to her mother every day and called her "my best friend."

"Some guy I knew in college," she said.

Britney nodded sagely. "A stalker. Why don't you just block his number?"

"Of course!" Lisa said. "I don't know why I didn't think of that."

Britney smiled. "It's a less dramatic solution."

Lisa spent the rest of the day in a state of trembling anger, reliving every shitty thing Suzanne had said and done that she could bring to mind. "Why can't you remember the good times?" Teddy once said. She couldn't remember any good times, only the bad: her constant criticism of Lisa's behavior and appearance; promises never kept. One never knew whether the ice of Suzanne's mood was thin or thick enough to test.

Finally she called Teddy again.

"Tell me a good time with Suzanne," she said.

"Nantucket?" he said. "That house Mom rented when you were ten and I was twelve?"

"I don't remember that."

"Sure you do. The house on Pine Street. Mom was great, she hardly drank at all. We used to ride our bikes to the beach and have a picnic every day. You were afraid of the waves. Mom would hold your hand and help you dive through the breakers. We'd go to the market on Main Street and buy flowers in the morning, and to the Sweet Shoppe for ice cream after dinner. You and Mom both loved strawberry. One day we went out in a sailboat. I remember being surprised Mom knew how to sail, but she did. We had a blast."

Lisa recalled the crashing waves and Suzanne's hand in hers; the blue horizon that sliced the ocean she imagined went on forever. "Watch the waves," Suzanne had said. "When you see the biggest one, the one that scares you most, hold your breath and dive under it." Beneath the wave, the water was bubbly but calm, and Lisa would bob to the surface like a buoy.

"Okay, thanks," she said to Teddy.

"You remember?" he said excitedly. "It's a good memory."

"It is," she said.

When she got home at the end of the day, she dumped her purse on the floor. She could see Rosie outside on the patio. Peter came out of his office.

"Your mother called."

"She called you?" Lisa said.

"No, she called the landline." As if bidden, the landline rang. "That would be her," Peter said. "She's been calling every thirty minutes all afternoon."

"Teddy must have given her that number too," Lisa said.

"Let it ring."

"No, she'll only keep calling."

"Then I'll leave it off the hook."

Peter picked up the phone and handed it to her. "Just tell her to stop."

"Hey sweetie!" Suzanne said in the same cheery voice, as if they spoke on the phone every day. "What are you doing right now?"

Lisa sat down at the kitchen counter in a fading patch of light. It was getting dark earlier these days; summer was winding down. "Right now?" she said.

"Yes," Suzanne said.

"Right now, I'm talking to you."

THE WEATHER OF MENOPAUSE

It was late, eleven o'clock, the end of a day in which Katrina had gotten nothing done, avoiding her studio in favor of the trifecta of time wasters, Facebook and Instagram and Twitter. Her husband, Gabriel, stood in front of the open closet in his boxers, hanging up the suit he had worn to his job as an entertainment attorney. Though men were said to age more gracefully than women, in Katrina's opinion that wasn't necessarily true. Most of the men she'd known since they were young were overweight or balding, often both, or unattractive in the first place and made more so by time. Gabe, however, had aged as beautifully as a piece of driftwood.

"I would be miserable if you had an affair," she said. She lay on their bed watching a rerun of *Downton Abbey*, wrapped in a fluffy white bathrobe. "But I want you to know that I would understand."

"I'm not going to have an affair," he said. He flicked a minute piece of lint off a pant leg. He had been out at a business dinner with a celebrity whose name Katrina had forgotten almost as soon as she'd heard it. After nearly twenty-five years, she was immune to Gabe's clients.

"But you could," she said. "I'm giving you permission."

"Stop it, would you? I don't want your permission."

"Because I know I've lost my looks."

"You make it sound as if you've misplaced them. Have you checked between the sofa cushions?"

"Don't tease." She slid down into the pillows. "It isn't fun being me. I had about twelve hot flashes today." There probably hadn't been twelve, or maybe there had; she lived in the weather of menopause these days, tropical 24/7. She adjusted her bathrobe to contain her lolling boobs. She wished she had a chest as flat as Lady Mary Crawley's, so she could wear a long strand of pearls without it sliding into her cleavage. She used to be so lovely that people stared at her, but middle age had sucked the female from her face and fattened her hips and breasts, so she resembled an effeminate man with a Mae West body, her uncle and mother combined. Gabe did legal work for a well-known actress the same age as Katrina who had managed to stay thin and youthful. It was with this actress that Katrina imagined Gabe having an affair. They were close friends, Katrina and the actress, whose name was Calliope Lasko. Several years ago, Calliope bought one of Katrina's paintings, which was subsequently admired by a movie director she was dating. The painting the director then bought caught the eye of one of his friends, then a friend of that friend bought a painting too, until eventually Katrina was selling paintings at a consistent clip and becoming rather well known herself. Now all manner of people bought her paintings—she was represented by galleries in New York and Los Angeles—but that it was Calliope to whom she owed her success was an itchy, irrefutable fact. Maybe she'd been destined to be successful anyway, but because of Calliope she would never know.

Gabe got into bed and opened his book. Katrina turned off the television. Too lazy to get up and put on a nightgown, she decided to sleep in her bathrobe. She didn't want to have sex with Gabe. Sex was a country from which she'd recently emigrated with no foreseeable plan to return.

"What do you think of Calliope?" she said.

"She's nice," Gabe said.

"No, I mean do you think she's still pretty?"

"People do," he said.

"I'm not talking about people," Katrina said. "I'm asking if you think so."

"Not anymore," he said. "She's far too thin, and I don't think that plastic surgeon did her any favors. He took all the character out of her face."

"You think so?" Katrina said happily. She reached for her own book on the nightstand, a biography of Lucian Freud, and perused the color plates of Freud's scabrous paintings of hideous naked people. A feather of doubt tickled her mind. Calliope was beautiful by anyone's standards. "I used to be as thin as Calliope."

"When you were young," Gabe said. "A fiftysomething woman shouldn't look like she was just released from a camp."

"That's a horrible way to put it." She was always shocked when he was crass. Most of the time he was a gentleman. She had often been told how lucky she was to be married to him, though as far as she knew, no one had ever told him he was lucky to be married to her. "Do you love me?" she said.

"Of course I love you."

Hearing him say he loved her was like having her back scratched: it felt so good she had to ask again. "Really and truly?"

He didn't look up from his book. "Really and truly."

She opened the drawer of the nightstand and shook from an amber vial two pale blue tablets that would ensure a dreamless sleep. Do you still think I'm pretty? she wanted to ask, knowing he would say yes, but decided a lie would be more dispiriting than the truth. She wished it was really as simple as running her hand between the cushions, as if her youth were a dime and a penny and a bent paperclip.

Next to cocktail hour, which she religiously observed, morning was Katrina's favorite time of day. She would sit by the studio window and nurse a skim cappuccino, watching the sunlight warming the neighborhood's rooftop water towers, peacefully scrolling through her favorite shopping sites on her iPad before her assistant, Jeremy, arrived. She was painting a series of abstract canvases in shades of gray that were so gigantic that she had to use a rolling ladder; Jeremy was in charge of pushing her around. He also stretched and gessoed her canvases, cleaned Katrina's pallets and brushes, and laid out tubes of paint. A fledgling painter himself, he was supposed to be learning from her for school credit. Learning what, Katrina couldn't imagine: though she had been painting and drawing all her life, she could not have articulated what any of it meant. But Jeremy was able to. When he talked about her influences and imagery and compositions, she tuned him out. She didn't want to know what she was doing. *Knowing would kill it,* she thought.

This morning, Jeremy shuffled in around eleven, his thick, shoulder-length hair falling into his eyes, his shoulders hunched. He wore the same thing he'd worn the last time she'd seen him: a ripped flannel shirt over a stretched-out white T-shirt and camouflage cargo pants splattered with paint. He was a stunningly unattractive boy, with a horsey, pock-marked face and snaggled gray teeth he kept hidden by never smiling. He worked for Katrina three days a week.

Her phone rang as Jeremy took off his formless dark coat. He picked it up before Katrina could. "Katrina Weldon's line, may I ask who's calling? Hmm, I'm not sure, she might have stepped out." He pretended to search the studio for Katrina in a pantomime Katrina observed with amusement. "It's Calliope," he said when he handed over the phone.

"When are you going to get rid of that cretinous boy?" Calliope said.

"Funny. He was just saying the nicest things about you," Katrina said.

"Listen, will you meet me for an early lunch?"

"I guess I can carve out some time," Katrina said, though she was pleased to have a reason to go out. Nevertheless, it pissed her off when people assumed she was available during the day.

They met at a restaurant across the street from Carnegie Hall, midway between Calliope's apartment on the Upper West Side and Katrina's studio in Chelsea. Katrina took the subway, Calliope a cab; they arrived at the restaurant at the same time. To show that she was too busy to think about her appearance, Katrina hadn't changed out of her painting clothes, black leggings and a knee-length black sweater. Calliope was impeccable in a tweed suit, her dark hair done up in a shining chignon. Katrina's hair was cut precisely at her chin and streaked blond so the gray would be less noticeable. Downtown she looked arty; uptown she looked eccentric.

"Why do you wear those eyeglasses?" Calliope said when they sat down. "They make you look like Harry Potter."

Katrina took off her glasses and looked at them. Framed in black plastic, perfectly round, she had paid a terrific amount for them at a trendy eyewear shop downtown. "These are the latest thing, you just don't know it," she said. She opened the menu, though she knew without looking that she would order the fettucine Alfredo. Calliope would order a salad or bowl of soup, which was why she was thin and Katrina wasn't. Screw it, Katrina thought, life was short. She ordered a glass of Chardonnay.

"Big news," Calliope said. "Huge news." She leaned forward as if she were imparting a secret and raised her left hand. A large diamond the shape of an egg twinkled on her ring finger. "I'm getting married."

"What?" Katrina said. "To whom?"

"Whom do you think?" Calliope said. "To Henrik, of

course!"

"Henrik from Vienna?"

"Why are you acting so surprised?" Calliope said. "You know we've been seeing each other for over a year."

"Long distance," Katrina said. "I mean, how many times have you actually seen him? You're not thinking of moving to Vienna?"

Calliope sat back. "Of course I'm moving to Vienna, I love Vienna. I've never been married and I want to be. I deserve a little domestic security at this point in my life, not to mention a dependable sex life." She smiled at the blushing busboy filling their water glasses who obviously recognized her. "Everything you have, in other words."

Katrina stared at her. "You can't."

Calliope sighed impatiently. "I can, and I'm going to. I thought you'd be happy for me, Katrina."

"I am happy for you," Katrina said.

"You don't look it," Calliope said. "Unless those are tears of joy, which I don't think they are."

Katrina bowed her head, dabbed her eyes with her napkin. "This sounds ridiculous, but I imagined you and Gabe would have an affair."

"What?" Calliope said. "Why?"

"Because if I imagine it, it won't happen."

"It wouldn't anyway!"

"No, no, I didn't really think it would. You were a stand-in. I can't explain, it made sense in my mind. I don't want him to have an affair, but I'm scared he will." She touched the nascent wattle at her throat. Maybe she should have plastic surgery. "If you consciously imagine something, it will never happen. Like imagining the plane crashing before you get on it. It's the things you don't think about that happen." The gabble of other conversations filled her ears; the crash of a dropped tray of plates came from the vicinity of the kitchen. A waiter arrived at their table and introduced himself as

Sean.

"I'll have the arugula salad," Calliope said without consulting the menu.

"The same," Katrina said.

"I can't even pretend to know what you're talking about," Calliope said.

"Never mind," Katrina said. "The tragic thing is I'll miss you terribly."

"You will," Calliope said with satisfaction. "Of course I'll miss you, too. And just so you know, Gabe's not my type."

"He's better looking than Henrik," Katrina said.

"You've met Henrik once," Calliope said. "I think you're jealous."

"Of what?" Katrina said. "I have everything you want, you said it yourself." When a little heap of glistening arugula arrived on a glass plate, she looked at it despondently. She had always felt slightly superior to Calliope with her peripatetic life, flitting from one man to the next, in and out of love, never seeing beneath the surface of anything, always just a little bit ridiculous. She remembered that Henrik was a baron. He'd behaved quite haughtily the time she met him.

"Will you be a baroness?" she said.

Calliope smiled. "Nobody uses the title, but yes. Isn't that a hoot?"

"Such a hoot," Katrina said.

According to the calculator on her phone, if a six-ounce glass of wine contained 144 calories, the three glasses a day that Katrina usually drank added up to 3,024 calories a week, 12,096 a month, 145,152 a year. Divided by 3500, which was the amount of calories that equaled a pound, she could conceivably lose forty-one pounds in a year if she didn't drink another glass of wine. She went to the refrigerator and counted the bottles of wine lying prone and uncorked on the bottom shelf. Four bottles, plus an open one on a shelf inside the door. What if she cut down to two glasses a day and skipped breakfasts? Or, still drank three, but skipped breakfast and ate only lettuce for lunch? She took the open bottle of Pinot Grigio out of the fridge and poured herself a glass. Obviously she couldn't go on the wagon until she'd finished the wine she had.

She stirred a pot of beef stew on the stove. Beef stew was the only really good thing she knew how to make. As well as the stew, she'd prepared scalloped potatoes; she'd found the recipe online that afternoon and sent Jeremy to buy the potatoes. Before he left for the evening, he'd asked if he could bring a few of his paintings to the studio for her *feedback,* a word she hated. She'd said okay because he'd gone out for the potatoes, which he'd had a perfect right to refuse to do, but she had no desire whatsoever to talk to him about his work. At this stage in her life she had only so many shits to give, and none of them were for Jeremy.

She settled down in the living room with a fresh glass of wine to watch the news. It was, as usual, shocking and depressing, so she surfed the channels until she found something intriguing: a dewy-skinned young woman twisting a hank of her hair around her finger and crying inconsolably. The word *nubile* flowered in Katrina's mind.

"He kissed me at the end of our date and said he wanted to see me again," the girl said. "Ashley isn't that pretty, I'm prettier than she is. I don't think she loves Kyle, I think she just wants him to choose her. I thought me and him were really good together."

"He and I!" Katrina shouted at the television. What idiots people were. She got up to check on the potatoes. Just as she closed the oven door, Gabe walked in.

"Perfect timing," she said.

He widened his eyes. "You're cooking dinner?"

"Why the face? I cook all the time."

"You order," he said. "Different."

"Either way, dinner is served."

Gabe opened a bottle of Merlot, and they sat down at the dining room table. Usually it was piled with books and papers and empty mail order boxes, a way station for all the crap they didn't want to immediately deal with. Tonight Katrina had cleared the mess and set the table with china she'd unearthed from their storage space in the basement of the building.

She ran her finger around the gilded rim of her plate. "Remember these?"

"You mean the plates?" Gabe said. "No, should I?"

"They're from our wedding china. We picked them out together."

He pushed his food aside and examined the plate's pattern of dinky pink flowers. "No way I picked this out. It looks like something my grandmother would have had."

"You did too," Katrina said. "We went to Tiffany and registered for them. I thought of them because our twenty-fifth anniversary is coming up." She put down her fork and clasped her hands beneath her chin. "I had the most marvelous idea. I think we should renew our vows."

Gabe opened his mouth but didn't say anything. Then he smiled. "Let's do. Let's quote soft-rock lyrics to each other under a floral arch at some cheesy Caribbean resort and make all our friends spend thousands of dollars to get there. It'll be so special, don't you think?" He laughed delightedly.

"I'm serious!" Katrina said. "I think it would be lovely. We could do it here, invite just a few close friends . . ." She had in fact been thinking of a ceremony at some island venue, an ocean breeze playing with the hem of her dress, a large audience of their friends looking on.

"What a nauseating idea," Gabe said. They sat in silence, eating their stew.

"It makes me sad," Katrina said after a while.

"What does?" Gabe said.

"That you find the idea of marrying me again nauseating. But of course you do, why wouldn't you? I'm hideous."

"Oh for God's sake, Katrina, stop it," Gabe said. "I didn't say you're hideous."

"But you think it," she said.

"No, but I tell you what I do think. I think you've had too much to drink."

Katrina looked at her half-empty glass. "Calliope is getting married to that Austrian baron."

"Is she? Ah. So that's what this is about," he said.

"No, it's not, I've been thinking about this for a long time." She hadn't thought of it until that afternoon. "It would be an opportunity to refresh our relationship." She reached out and caressed his cheek, his five o'clock shadow rasping the back of her hand.

His phone vibrated. "I have to take this," he said. He stood and walked away from the table. "No, not at all," Katrina heard him say from the living room before the conversation devolved into a murmur. She drained her glass, poured herself another, and sipped it while she waited for him to return. After fifteen minutes, she went into the living room. He was watching a movie on TV.

"Let's have sex," she said.

He looked up at her. "You're drunk," he said. "Go to bed."

She stared at him. He stared at the TV. What she needed, she thought, was a dog.

She had a poisonous hangover she'd hidden from Gabe by leaving for the studio while he was still in the shower. Drinking a large cappuccino with an extra shot of espresso, she scrolled blearily through pictures of Morkie puppies. A Morkie would be adoring and fit in a bag so she could take it wherever she wanted, like one of those little oxygen tanks old people carried when they were forced to be out in the world. She'd had a cocker spaniel as a child, a nasty biter, that ultimately had to be euthanized because it attacked a neighborhood child. She put her head down on her worktable and wondered if she would vomit. She felt a hand on her back. The room reeled as she sat up.

"Katrina? Are you okay?" Jeremy said.

"Of course I am. I'm just thinking is all. What are you doing here, Jeremy? Today's not your day."

"Yes, it is. We changed my schedule, remember?"

She had no memory whatsoever of changing Jeremy's days. "Oh, yes, of course. But I don't need you today. You can go."

Beneath his dark coat, Jeremy's body seemed to sag. "But I brought in my paintings for you to look at."

"Right!" Katrina said. She did remember that.

He shouldered out of his coat and began to extricate the paintings from layers of plastic bubble wrap and packing tape. "These are from this semester," he said excitedly. "I think I've hit a groove, you know? For the first time, I feel I have some control now instead of just throwing paint around and wondering, What the hell."

"Well, what the hell goes with the territory," Katrina said. "You don't want to lose that entirely." She wondered if she could ask him to go out and get her another coffee. He was smiling for once, showing his awful teeth. He must have come from a background where orthodontia wasn't a priority.

"Tell me, Jeremy, what do your parents think of you pursuing a career in art?"

"They're totally against it," he said. "I haven't seen them since I moved here. They're like, come home when you're ready to do something with your life."

Katrina nodded. "Where are you from?"

"Fulton, Missouri. You've never heard of it."

"No, I haven't," she admitted. Come to think of it, she wasn't even sure of Jeremy's last name. James or Jones, something alliterative and simple. "Okay, let's see your paintings."

He began again to unwrap them. One emerged, then another, finally a third. "It's a triptych," he said shyly. "They're meant to go together."

"I can see that," she said.

"What do you think?" His face was pale, his jaw set as if braced for a blow.

She rolled her chair closer to examine each, and then rolled away to view them as a whole. They were a study in controlled chaos, the strokes of the brush sure and bold and glowing with exuberance, connecting here and breaking there, bridges and rivers and highways of color in magical combinations. The paintings hit a satisfying spot, brought forth a recognition. They reached a destination that had eluded her for thirty years. He was terribly gifted, this Jeremy James or Jones. She had never thought very deeply about her work, but she recognized what she didn't have.

"You don't really have to be all that talented, Jeremy, you just have to be lucky," she said. She took her wallet out of her purse and handed him a ten. "Go get us a couple of coffees, will you?"

He looked at his paintings; he looked at her. He took the money and left. When she heard the ping of the elevator door, she wished she'd asked him to get her a muffin.

EVEN-STEVEN

"They say I'm dying," my stepmother said. Her voice on the phone was gravelly from forty-plus years of smoking. *Dying for what?* was my first thought because she was always "dying" for something, usually a cocktail or a cigarette.

"Who says you're dying, Bree?"

"My team of doctors at Sloan Kettering," she said. "Apparently I have cancer. Riddled with it, in fact. They tell me I'll be dead in a few weeks."

"What? No. How long has this been going on?"

"Ages, probably, silently spreading. I'd been feeling sort of crappy, so I went to my doctor last week. Before I knew it, I was in the hospital having the most horrible tests. There's one where they put you into a tube that makes an outrageous racket, bang-bang-bang, I thought I'd lose my mind. Anyway, long story short I have tumors everywhere—bones, brain, liver, you name it. They want me to go to a hospice to die." She said "hospice" in a tone of deep disgust. She was a terrible snob.

"I'm so sorry, Bree," I said. I was. Bree and I weren't close, but since my father died a few years ago, we had maintained a relationship that consisted of sporadic phone calls and occasional meals together. I resented and liked her; she seemed to feel the same about me. It was an uneasy combination, but we managed to get along.

"Thank you for saying so," she said. "I'm sorry too. Fifty-nine is far too young to shuffle off this mortal coil, but there it is, nothing to do about it."

"Have you told Charlotte?" I said. Charlotte was my stepsister, Bree's only child.

"I would if I could get a hold of her, but I can't, her number is disconnected. I'll hear from her when she wants money. She'd bankrupt me if she could. The only thing is, I might be dead before then." Bree was allowed to say shitty things about Charlotte, but she would turn on me like a viper if I so much as nodded in agreement. Charlotte was a junkie. The single thing we had in common was we were the same age, thirty-two. The last I heard she lived on Delancey Street with a fellow junkie named Monty, but I'd never known her to stay anywhere for more than a few months before getting into some drama, personal or financial, that necessitated seeking out new fellow junkies and some other ratty place to live.

"I could try to find her, if you'd like," I said before I knew it. I didn't know how I would do that. I hadn't seen her in a year. I imagined hiring a private eye like a character in the movies.

"It would be awfully nice if you did. Why don't you come over for a drink tonight? Are you free?"

"Sure, yes," I said. I was free practically all the time since my husband left me six weeks earlier. Concurrently, I had been laid off from my job as an arborist at the Central Park Conservancy, so I was at liberty both night and day, buoyed by unemployment checks and a tiny inheritance from my father. New York City had always been my home, but it had a limited number of trees. I knew I would have to leave it sooner or later if I wanted to find another job in my field.

"Don't bring Brad," Bree said. "I want it to be just us."

"Okay." I hadn't told her about Brad's defection. I doubted I would. I was embarrassed because he'd left me for our downstairs neighbor, another reason I needed to move. "Can I bring a bottle of wine? Some cheese and crackers?"

"No, nothing."

"But I don't want you to go to any trouble."

"Don't be silly," she said. "I'm not in the least infirm. You'd never know I'm at death's door if I hadn't told you."

I was twenty-two and in my final year of college when my father married Bree, only five months after my mother died of Parkinson's disease. I was certain they had been having an affair while my mother was still alive, and as my father and I had never agreed about anything, I saw as little of them as I could. It was only since he died of a heart attack that I had made an effort to be friendly to Bree. I knew she was lonely without him and missed seeing Charlotte, whom she adored despite all. Though I owed her less than nothing, I felt sorry for her.

I had grown up in what was now Bree's apartment, and it still retained a very particular odor—cigarettes, soap, the musk of old rugs—that brought me back to my childhood. I fell into a chair by the empty fireplace and accepted a martini from Bree. She had lost an alarming amount of weight and there was a greenish tinge to her skin; her cheekbones were sharp, her eyes deep in their sockets. She had gotten dressed up in a pert salmon-colored suit I recognized from when it fit her. I was wearing a turtleneck that was too heavy for the warm December evening. I ran my finger around its sweaty neck and thought gloomily about global warming.

"I knew your mother, you know," Bree said as she sat down across from me. "Well, no, I can't say I knew her, but I met her a few times. She was lovely. You have her green eyes. I don't think she liked me."

"Why do you think that?" I said.

"Oh, probably because I was sleeping with your father. Of course she knew it, she wasn't stupid. Neither are you."

"I hated you and Dad for that," I said.

"Naturally you did, you loved your mother, and it was a terrible thing for us to do. I didn't much care about people's feelings in those days. I hope I'm a little bit better now." She opened an enameled box on the table beside her and took out a cigarette. She lit it, inhaled deeply, and blew out a fierce stream of smoke. "I wonder if I'll to Heaven or Hell."

"You don't believe in any of that," I said. As far as I knew, she didn't go to church.

"I don't know what I believe. I've never thought seriously about an afterlife until now. I didn't expect to die prematurely—though why not? People do. Your father did."

"So did my mother."

"What, if anything, do you believe?"

"I believe in reincarnation."

"Ah, karma," she said. "In that case you might be reborn as my wicked stepmother." She coughed wetly and pounded her chest with her fist. "I wasn't very nice to you when your father was alive."

"I wasn't very nice to you."

"Shall we call it even?"

"Even-steven." I felt pleasantly tipsy from the martini. Bree had put out a dish of almonds; I took a few and crunched in silence. "Brad and I split up," I said.

"Excellent news!" she said. "I never liked that man, I thought he was a dick masquerading as a darling. So, so pleasant, but you could see the nasty thoughts in his eyes. He wasn't good enough for you. That was clear from the start."

"I didn't know you thought that."

"Oh, yes. Your father thought so too."

Immediately, I felt released from the pain and humiliation Brad had inflicted on me. *You're not good enough for me!* I imagined shouting at him, though sadly it was too late for that.

"I'm thinking of looking for another job," I said. "Maybe moving out of the city."

Bree's tired eyes, tinged yellow, went wide with surprise. "Well, look at you, making great strides! I'd say I'll miss you when you're gone, but I won't be here either. You couldn't have chosen a better time as far as I'm concerned."

I had to laugh. "That was my plan all along."

"Listen," she said. "I'm not going to go to an awful hospice. I'm going to die right here in my bed. I've hired a nurse to take care of me during the daytime. That's all I can afford, I'm afraid. Would you mind looking in on me in the evenings? I can try to find someone else if need be. I know it's a lot to ask."

"Absolutely," I said. It was the last thing I wanted to do. I had no experience with death, having been at college when my mother passed away in her sleep and at work when my father had his heart attack. I was terrified of death and didn't want to be anywhere near it.

"Oh, thank you so much," she said. She clasped her hands together, her rings sliding loose on her fingers. "I don't think I'll linger long. Speaking of which . . ." Shakily, she got up and retrieved her gigantic handbag from a table in the front hall. I was surprised she had the strength to carry it. From its depths she excavated a creased yellow Post-it. "I sent a check to Charlotte at this address about two months ago, and I know she received it because she cashed it." She handed me the Post-it.

I read the downtown address. "Hopefully she's still there," I said. I wasn't going to make any promises.

"I can't tell you what it would mean to me to see her," Bree said. I looked up at her. Her eyes were glassy with tears. I had never seen her so vulnerable before.

The building was a brick tenement in the no-man's-land west of SoHo, near the Holland Tunnel. Soot from the exhaust of rush hour traffic dulled the windowpanes, and the pale marble steps to the sidewalk were worn concave from years of use. But the foyer was tidy, its green walls freshly painted, the brass mailboxes unmolested. I buzzed the apartment number written on the Post-it and was immediately let in. A woman was waiting at the apartment door.

"I thought you were someone else," she said. She was dressed in black pants and a white men's shirt, her brown hair pulled back into a bun.

"I have the wrong place," I said. "I thought my stepsister Charlotte lived here."

"She did," the woman said. "About two months back. She was sleeping on my couch."

I frowned at her, confused. I didn't have to say what I was thinking for her to understand.

"I've been clean for seventeen months and thirteen days," she said stoutly. "I have a good job in catering. Charlotte was clean too while she was here. Come in, I don't want to stand out here. The lady next door is an eavesdropper." She beckoned for me to follow her. We went down a hall to a sparsely furnished room. There was couch, a hard chair, and a table on which sat a short stack of library books and a spiral ring binder. She sat on the couch; I took the chair. "I'm Madison. You're Charlotte's sister? You don't look alike."

"Stepsister," I said. "We're not actually related."

"Oh. Well, as I say, she was clean, so I let her stay with me. She was doing good, too, going to NA with me, trying to find work. But after a couple of weeks she started using again. Hey, where are my manners, would you like a glass of water?" She sprang up and went into a kitchenette and came back with two glasses of water. She took a sip of hers and sat down again, putting the glass on the floor by her feet. "I came home one night after work and she was high. She tried to act like she wasn't, but her kit was sitting right there on the table. I let her stay until the morning, then I asked her to leave. I had to," she said as if I had challenged her. "I have my own sobriety to consider. It's not easy. I don't need any temptation."

"I understand," I said.

"Neither of us is getting any younger, and I'm five years younger than her. I said, 'What, do you want to be a junkie all your life?'"

"What did she say?"

"She said it was just a one-time thing. But it's always just a one-time thing, then it's another, and another. Believe me, I know. I do think she wants to get clean, I give her credit for that, but it might be beyond her ability."

"Do you ever see her?" I said. "I need to talk to her. Her mother is dying."

Madison shook her head. "I'm sorry, I don't. I don't want to, either. I'm trying to better myself. I'm taking an accounting class at Baruch. I'm good with numbers, or I used to be. Heroin sucks the smarts right out of your brain." She looked out the filthy window. Her cheeks were marred by small scars. I thought she looked used up for someone so young, any spark she'd once had long extinguished. "I know who might be in touch with her, though. That steakhouse called Americana on Varick Street? There's a guy named Frank who's the manager there. He's been sober for years. He has a soft spot for Charlotte. Sometimes he gives her free meals. He might know where she's living."

I had never known Charlotte when she wasn't taking drugs—pot, which I had shared with her more than once, speed and cocaine, and finally the heroin that swallowed her whole. She hadn't much to fall back on. She wasn't smart or pretty or gifted; when I met her, she'd just dropped out of community college and was temping as a receptionist at a law firm. She had a dopey kind of cheerfulness in the early days, always glad to shoot the breeze with whoever happened to cross her path. The last time I saw her was Christmas, a year ago, when she'd showed up at Bree's apartment with a chipped front tooth and track marks on both arms. Speaking only when spoken to, she'd played with her dinner and left immediately afterward. "Wasn't it great to see Charlotte?" Bree had said as we cleared the dishes. I pretended I hadn't heard.

I walked the few blocks to Americana, which was empty and dim at that time of day, the dark paneled walls closing in. Red tinsel was haphazardly tacked up around the door to the restroom, and plastic holly decorated the tables. I sat down at the bar and asked the bartender if I could talk to Frank.

"Come back in an hour," he said. "He usually gets in around five."

"I'll wait," I said, and ordered a Chardonnay. The two TVs suspended above the bar were broadcasting a football game. The sound was off, but just the sight of the game was enough to make me chew on disturbing thoughts of Brad, who was an idiot fan of the Giants. At five-thirty, I ordered a second glass and told myself I would only wait as long as it took to drink it. I'd expected to reach a dead end at the address Bree gave me, not be sent on a lengthy hunt.

"What do you want Frank for, anyway?" the bartender said. He looked too young to drink alcohol, never mind serve it.

"I was hoping he might be able to tell me where my stepsister Charlotte is living."

He gaped at me. "I know Charlotte. Or knew her. I heard she died."

"What? When? How? Heard from who?"

"Frank told me a while ago. He was really upset about it. She got some bad stuff, he said."

"Stuff?" I said. I knew what he meant. "How does Frank know?"

"You'll have to ask him."

"Charlotte's mother is dying!" I felt a little hysterical. "I don't know how I'm going to tell her about this." Goddamn you, Charlotte, I thought. I was too mad to feel sorry.

"That sucks," he said. "My condolences."

I was sick of waiting, so I got up and left. I'd done what I'd been asked to do.

Bree's teeth became her prominent feature as the rest of her wasted away. She was so skeletal that I was afraid I would break her bones as I sat her up to give her a pill or maneuvered her over a bedpan, a thing I had never imagined I would do. She was taking painkillers and mostly slept. Lying on the upholstered chaise in her room, I would try to sleep myself, but alert to every noise she made, I was only able to doze. She coughed and sighed and mumbled and had spates where her breath came in bursts. The nurse who took care of her during the day believed that Bree was being visited in her sleep by loved ones from the "other side."

"They're helping her to pass over," she said after one particularly restless night. "It's not easy to die, it takes some doing." Her name was Hedda and she specialized in caring for the terminally ill. She sang hymns under her breath.

"You mean the other side as in Heaven," I said.

"I don't know what the other side is," she said. "I only know it exists. I've seen patients reach out and speak the name of a deceased loved one, and I believe they're being called to pass over."

I hoped that wasn't true. I hadn't told Bree about Charlotte. I couldn't bear to, so I had put it off and said I was still looking.

"Where do you think she is?" she said one evening as the painkiller was kicking in.

"I heard she got a job in California." It was the first thing that came to my mind.

"A job!" Bree said with childlike wonder. "What kind of job?"

"Well, you know how good she is with people . . ."

"She is! She really is."

"The friend of hers I spoke to said she's working in human resources."

"That's perfect for her," Bree said. "Why haven't you called her?"

"Oh, I have," I said. "I left a message this afternoon. I expect she'll call back any moment." I knew that by tomorrow Bree would have forgotten. She wasn't herself anymore.

But one morning she woke early and called to me in her gravelly old voice. I started up immediately and went to her bed. The room was filled with dawn.

"What do you need?" I said. She patted the bed. I sat down beside her.

"Why are you being so good to me?" she said. She was as lucid as if she were well.

"What do you see when you're sleeping?" I said.

"See?"

"Dream."

"I don't remember. Why?"

"Hedda thinks you're seeing your dead loved ones."

"Well, I'm not," she said flatly. She sighed and looked at her desiccated hands. "Your father had the right idea. Bang, he was dead. I told you I wouldn't linger, but it seems I am."

"Linger as long as you like," I said.

"Have you heard anything about Charlotte?"

"I found an old roommate of hers."

"And?"

"Charlotte got clean," I said. "But then she relapsed."

"What a terrible drug heroin is," Bree said.

"It is," I said. It was the first time we'd ever spoken openly about Charlotte's addiction. "I'm sorry about Charlotte.

I've never been able to tell you that. She was fun, so nice. I liked her a lot."

"I don't suppose I'll see her before I die," Bree said sadly.

"Don't think that," I said. She would see Charlotte soon enough, I thought. I felt I had been right not to tell her.

"You know, it's the oddest thing, I don't feel any pain right now."

"That is odd," I said. "Nothing? Nowhere?" She shook her head. We sat for a moment, considering this development. I didn't know what to think.

"I'll miss this life," she said. "I've enjoyed myself. I'm not ready to die." She reached for the water glass on the nightstand beside her bed. I picked it up and gave it to her, helped her take a sip through the straw. "You and I have just gotten started, really. I wish we'd been friends before." When she smiled, I had to look away, her skeleton's face was so frightening.

"In the next life," I said. "I'll see you there."

She raised the water glass with trembling hands. "To the next life," she said.

The doorbell rang. "That'll be Hedda," I said.

"Oh, Hedda," Bree said. "If I hear 'Nearer My God to Thee' one more time, I'll find a gun and shoot myself."

I laughed and went to get Hedda. "She's very sharp this morning," I said as I opened the door. Charlotte stood in the hall.

"Hi," she said.

I put my hand to my heart. "Charlotte! My God, come in. Where have you been? Someone told me you died."

"I almost did," she said. "I was dead for eleven minutes. I've been in rehab. I just got out. I called Madison, she told me about Mom." I studied her eyes. She wasn't high. But she was bedraggled. She wore jeans that looked as if they belonged to someone else, and a hairy brown sweater that was unraveling at the shoulder. Her dark blond hair needed to be washed, but she smelled okay, and her skin was clear of blemishes.

"Your mom is awake," I said. "You need to go in and see her."

"I'm sorry I couldn't come before," she said. "I didn't know."

"She's lucid right now," I said.

"Got it." She started down the hall to Bree's room.

"Wait." I unbuttoned the pink cardigan I was wearing. "Let's trade." She took off her sweater and put on mine. "And take this," I said as I unclasped my silver chain necklace.

She put the chain around her neck. "Can I borrow your barrette too?" She pulled back her hair and clipped it neatly into the barrette. The sight of her doing that ordinary thing made me feel like weeping with gratitude.

"Let me see you," I said. The cardigan cast a rosy glow on her face and brightened her gray-blue eyes. "Okay, go on in." I waited until she entered Bree's bedroom, then gathered my things and left. I passed Hedda on the street.

"You left her alone?" she said in an alarmed voice. Her breath turned to smoke in the frigid air.

"Her daughter is with her," I said.

"I thought you were her daughter."

"No, just a friend."

"So, you're off the hook," she said.

The remark annoyed me. I had never complained. Being needed was more seductive than being loved. For the first time in my life, I was neither.

YOU HAVE REACHED YOUR DESTINATION

Amelia's older brother had a heart attack. *Of course he did*, Amelia thought. Glenn smoked a pack of Marlboros a day. The only mystery was when it would happen. So it happened. He survived.

"Amazing," Amelia said.

"What is?" said Glenn's wife, Betsy, who phoned on Wednesday with the news.

"That he isn't dead," Amelia said.

"Well, he isn't," Betsy said. "Are you coming down to see him?"

"To Baltimore?" Amelia said.

"Yes, to Baltimore," Betsy said. "Because that is where we live. You haven't been down here in years. In a decade, I bet."

Almost exactly a decade, not since her mother died, though Betsy and Glenn visited Amelia in New York now and then. Glenn had three children, to whom Amelia dutifully gave Christmas presents Betsy picked out and wrapped, but she didn't like children and she didn't like Baltimore, and she wasn't fascinated by Glenn and Betsy, either. Glenn was good-natured, everyone's best friend. If he had died, his funeral would have been standing room only, featuring sentimental eulogies and a profusion of flowers. At least Amelia had been spared that. She'd given a eulogy once in her life, for a college friend who'd drowned; she'd felt like an actress playing a woman giving a eulogy, hollow and pretentious, a phony.

She took the train to Baltimore on Friday afternoon and was met at the station by a young woman who wore jeans and a T-shirt that read "Bertha's Mussels," the letters stretched wide across her breasts.

"Aunt Amelia? It's Debbie."

"Debbie!" Amelia said. "I didn't recognize you."

Debbie laughed. "Then it's a good thing I recognized you." She led Amelia to a dusty blue Beetle and drove them north past bleak blocks of derelict row houses, corner stores, empty lots strewn with garbage, makeshift community churches.

"It's always been like this," Amelia said.

Debbie nodded. "Yeah, it's pretty rough."

"Why do you live here?" Amelia said.

"Oh, I don't live downtown."

"No, I mean why do you live in Baltimore?"

"Where else should I live?"

"I don't know. New York, Los Angeles, Chicago. You're an adult now. What are you, twenty-three? You can live anywhere you like."

Debbie regarded Amelia out of the corner of her eye. She was compact and curvaceous, plump but firm. Her skin was too evenly tanned to have gotten that way from the sun. Her eyes were Glenn's, blue and slightly bulging, and she had her mother's riotous blond curls. "My brothers live in D.C.," she said, as if that made up for the fact that she'd stayed.

Soon the slums gave way to a wide parkway that eventually spilled into a dense, tree-lined neighborhood of modest brick houses. Glenn's colonial sat on a grassy rise above a short flight of cement steps from the street.

"Jesus it's hot," Amelia said to no one. Debbie had parked the car and gone ahead. Amelia had forgotten how she'd suffered during the summers here, the suffocating humidity and prickly heat rashes, whole afternoons spent submerged in the YMCA pool.

Betsy came out of the house. She'd cut her hair very short since the last time Amelia saw her, and she was carrying a tire of flab above the waistband of her slacks. She had been stunning when she was young, miles out of Glenn's league, but somehow he'd convinced her to let him take her out and then, more surprising, to marry him. Amelia supposed they had been happy, or happy enough. She had never been married and hadn't wanted to be. The drama that invaded long-term relationships annoyed her to the point of disgust. When she wanted sex, she phoned a number that connected her through a discreet service with a young man called Lance, whose last name she didn't know or care to know; she'd grown tired of him lately and planned to request someone new.

"Glenn's in the family room watching the Orioles," Betsy said as she kissed Amelia's cheek. "He insisted on getting out of bed for your arrival, but don't let him get excited—he really should be resting. He looks like hell. I wanted to prepare you."

"'Like hell' sounds pretty dire," Amelia said.

"You'll see," Betsy said. "Go on in and say hello. He's thrilled you came down."

Inside the house, the window shades were drawn against the afternoon heat. Wiping a mustache of perspiration from her lip, Amelia followed the familiar sound of a baseball game, the crack of the bat and the cheering crowd, announcer's relentless commentary.

Glenn was sitting in a recliner, next to a growling window unit. He turned and smiled. His face was grayish white, bloodless. In contrast, his teeth looked shockingly yellow. He was wearing a pale blue terry cloth robe and a pair of old loafers. His bare legs were hairless and spotted and thin. He struggled to get up, but Amelia went to him before he could stand and hugged him awkwardly around his neck. Betsy was right; he did look like hell.

"What's the score?"

"The O's are down," Glenn said. "I was hoping they'd make the playoffs, but it looks like they won't even get close. How are you doing, Amy?"

"I should be asking you that," Amelia said.

"I'm bored out of my mind, and I'd give my last dime for a cigarette. Tell me something new! I'm sick of myself."

"There's not much to tell. Work is crazy as usual." Amelia worked in advertising for a company that had offices all over the world. She traveled two weeks out of the month and would have been in Berlin now if Glenn hadn't had his heart attack. She sat down in an easy chair facing the recliner. The room was small and crowded with furniture, much of it from their late parents' house. There was a pine side table whose legs had been viciously chewed by a beagle they'd had as children, and a fake cherry veneer grandfather clock that Amelia remembered her mother ordering from a catalog.

"That clock doesn't run anymore," she said. "Look, it's frozen at ten fifteen. I can't believe you kept it. It's a piece of junk."

Glenn loosened the sash of his bathrobe and tied it again more tightly. "I have fond memories, that's why I kept it."

Amelia raised her eyes to the ceiling, where a small iron chandelier dangled from a cord. It had hung over her parents' dining room table, perennially dusty, casting anemic light on their food. "You took every last little thing of theirs, didn't you?" she said.

"You didn't want any of it," Glenn said.

"That's not the point," Amelia said.

"There's a point?"

Amelia looked away. She hadn't wanted their parents' things, but it irritated her that Glenn had. Part of what had driven her away thirty-five years ago was their parents' unapologetic mediocrity, but here was Glenn preserving their crappy stuff as if they were reminders of something enchanted. There had been nothing enchanted about their childhood. Their father had openly carried on with a variety of women—Amelia's fifth grade teacher had been one of them—and their mother had meted out her anger on Amelia and Glenn while being delightful to everyone else, including their father, which had been another reason to flee as soon as possible. Why didn't Glenn remember? Or if he did remember, why did he pretend? Amelia gazed at a painting of the Leaning Tower of Pisa on the wall that used to hang in their parents' living room. Why that hideous picture of all the pictures they could have chosen? They had never even been to Italy.

On TV, the crowd roared. A player dropped his bat and jogged around the diamond.

"Hot damn, a home run!" Glenn said. He smiled at Amelia with his yellow teeth, more excited than was good for him.

The bookshelf in the family room was full of popular junk, whodunits and romance novels, as well as an intriguing little chunk of self-help books: *The Seven Habits of Highly Effective People, The Power of Now, Living Beyond Fear, The Joys of Imperfection,* and *You Are A Badass: How To Stop Doubting Your Greatness.* Betsy managed alumni affairs for a private girls' school; Glenn sold insurance. How much greatness was there to doubt?

"Those are Dad's," Debbie said from the doorway. The house was quiet. Glenn was still asleep at half-past-eleven. The excitement of Amelia's arrival yesterday had exhausted him, Betsy said. Debbie joined Amelia by the bookshelf. Today she was wearing a pink and green flowered halter dress that was so tight it looked like it hurt. Amelia hadn't brought anything but a couple of blouses and the skirt she'd worn on the train. "That's what you're wondering, isn't it? Whose books they are?"

"Not yet, but I would have," Amelia said.

"He buys them, but he doesn't read them." Debbie pulled out *The Joys of Imperfection* and ran her finger along its uncracked spine. "I doubt he'd take any of the advice in these books even if he did read them. Dad's got low self-esteem, Mom says. He's a people pleaser. Smoking is literally the only thing he does purely for his own pleasure."

"And it almost killed him," Amelia said. "I doubt he's pleased about that."

Debbie bowed her head and hugged the book against her chest, her face clenching like a fist. Amelia realized she was crying. "Oh don't!" she said in a panicked voice. She couldn't remember the last time she'd seen someone cry. "Your dad will be back to his old self very soon, I'm sure."

"No, he won't," Debbie said. "His heart is damaged. The doctor said it's been weakened so much that he'll never be well."

Amelia sat down in Glenn's recliner and ran her hands over its grimy leather arms. A lifetime of Old Spice breathed from the headrest. She used to tease Glenn about wearing too much. "I don't have any family but Glenn," she said.

Debbie dabbed her eyes with the back of her wrist and blew her nose with a tissue she took from a shapeless leather purse. "What do you mean? You have us."

"You hardly know me."

"Doesn't matter, you're still my aunt. I can get to know you. Hey, why don't we go out to lunch together?"

"That sounds nice," Amelia said absently. That Glenn wouldn't get well hadn't crossed her mind. She felt her heart skip. She checked the pulse in her neck. Nothing, a normal beat.

"I mean right now," Debbie said.

"Now? Where?" Amelia said.

"Wherever!" Debbie said. She grabbed Amelia's hands and dragged her out of the recliner. Though tears still glistened on her cheeks, she looked as happy as a child.

"Wherever" turned out to be a low concrete building that had a neon Budweiser sign in its single window. Though it was around the corner from the neighborhood where Amelia grew up, she'd never been inside. Debbie pulled into a lot beside the building and sprang out of the car. She dropped her purse on the pavement between her feet and fluffed up her curls with both hands. She'd meant to come here all along, Amelia realized, even if she'd had to come alone.

"Debbie, this is a bar," she said.

"Yeah, but it's the coolest bar in Baltimore! Everyone comes here. They have great burgers. It's nicer inside than it looks."

It wasn't nice inside. It was so dark that Amelia could hardly see where she was going, and there was an overwhelming odor of stale beer. They sat down at a varnished wooden table that felt sticky to the touch. There were several people at other tables; a few of them waved at Debbie. The bartender looked about Debbie's age, his sullen face shadowed in the light from a glass fixture above the bar.

"Your boyfriend?" Amelia said, cocking her head toward the bar. She couldn't think why else they would be here.

"Who, Jackson? Not on your life," Debbie said. "Like I'd ever go out with a bartender."

Amelia smiled. "With whom would you go out?"

"Somebody rich. I don't want to be like my parents. You know, living in a shitty little house in a just-okay neighborhood. I want to live in the Valley in one of those big old houses, be a member of the country club out there."

Amelia sat back in surprise. She hadn't thought of Glenn's house as shitty. She'd always thought it was rather sweet, but she saw it now as Debbie did, a house not unlike the one she had grown up in and chafed to escape.

Jackson came over. Amelia ordered a Diet Coke.

"A Heineken and a shot of Cuervo," Debbie said. "Hey, you know what? Make that two shots."

"No thanks, I don't drink during the day," Amelia said.

"Not for you, for me."

Amelia raised her eyebrows.

"It's Saturday," Debbie said. "I'm allowed."

Amelia's father had been a heavy drinker. Drunk people made her nervous. You never knew what stupid thing they would do. She weighed whether or not to tell Debbie to slow down, but in the order of things she wanted to say, it seemed the least important. "Why do you think you have to depend on a man to get you the things you want?" she said. "Why not get a business degree and make your own money?"

"I suck at school, I wouldn't get through the first semester of an MBA. Besides, I want children, a family, the traditional stay-at-home-mom thing." She downed a shot of tequila and gazed out the window with the Budweiser sign as if something fascinating was happening beyond it. Outside, two women were talking on the sidewalk in front of the bar. Across the street was an auto mechanic's garage, and beyond it, the tall twin steeples of the Cathedral of St. Mary Our Queen, where Amelia and Glenn had endured the nuns from kindergarten through fifth grade. After a curiously long time, Debbie turned back to her. "I have gay friends. My college roommate was a lesbian."

What an odd thing to say, Amelia thought. Then it dawned on her. "I'm not gay, Debbie. Is that what you think? Why, because I never married? That's a pretty silly assumption to make."

"I'm not assuming anything! Grammy told me you're gay. She said that was why you moved away from Baltimore, because you were afraid of what people would think."

"Grammy was lying," Amelia said. "I left town to get

away from her, and she knew it. What a dreadful woman she was."

"Don't say that! I loved Grammy. Dad loved Grammy, too."

"Your father is in denial about your grandmother. If he lacks self-esteem, it's because of her. She treated him terribly when we were growing up."

Debbie looked at Amelia suspiciously. "Dad never said that." She drained her second shot, finished her beer, and raised her hand to get Jackson's attention. Amelia understood she came here often, despite her grand ambitions. Had she fucked Jackson? Amelia didn't doubt it. Debbie was her grandfather reincarnated. One of the women from the sidewalk came in and sat at the bar. Up close, she looked like a prostitute, makeup thick as spackle and teased-up yellow hair. Amelia used to pick up men in bars. Long ago. She wouldn't be caught dead now, on the cusp of fifty, sitting alone at a bar.

"Two burgers, please," Amelia said when Jackson came over.

"No food, the cook quit last week," Jackson said. He looked at Debbie. "You knew that."

"Oops, I forgot," Debbie said with a sly grin. "Well, they used to have great burgers." She propped her elbows on the table, framing her deep cleavage with her forearms. "Come on, have a drink, Aunt Amelia, don't be so uptight. I figured you'd be cool, being from New York and all. But that was when I thought you were gay. I bet you are gay, though, queer as a three-dollar bill, 'cause Grammy wasn't a liar, and neither is Dad."

"Your father never told you I'm gay," she said, though for all she knew, Glenn believed it too.

"No, I guess not," Debbie admitted. She seemed to deflate a little.

"Just the check, please," Amelia said to Jackson.

"When we'd go over to Grammy's, she'd make us German chocolate cake," Debbie said, gathering herself again. "And at Christmas she'd pretend Santa came to her house, too, so me and my brothers would get two stockings. She was the best."

"Your grandmother was a narcissistic bitch," Amelia said. She took her wallet out of her purse and gave Jackson two tens, waving away the change.

"*You're* a bitch," Debbie said. "Grammy was fantastic. She was the most amazing, kind, perfect human being I ever knew." She fished her ring of keys out of her purse and dangled them on the tip of her finger. Amelia noticed for the first time that her eye teeth were crooked, each overlapping the tooth beside it, reaching for its sister. "I'm the driver, remember? We're not leaving until I say so, and I want another drink."

"You're already too drunk to drive," Amelia said. The hot stench of tequila hovered between them, an invisible nimbus amidst the general funk of the bar. She reached for the keys, but Debbie snatched them away. Amelia honestly didn't care whether Debbie drove or not. She probably drove drunk all the time.

The trees were tall now on Dunston Lane, casting dappled blue shade on proud lawns; the ornamental shrubs, azalea and rhododendron, were so lush their leaves seemed polished. The modest houses that had been built in the seventies—thought of as "modern" when Amelia was a kid—had settled snugly into the landscape as if they had always been there, but Amelia remembered when the trees were so spindly they were anchored by wires, and the houses sat on their identical plots as if dropped, ready-made, from above. As the Uber approached the junction of Dunston and Belleview, she told the driver to slow down. She hunkered forward and watched through the windshield as a low white brick home came into view.

"Stop," she said. She rolled down her window. The shutters were deep blue instead of black, and the copper beech had grown so high it shaded most of the lawn. Where her mother had planted pink and white impatiens on either side of the stone path each spring, someone else had put in a jungle of ferns in shades of silvery green. The box bushes that flanked the front door were huge, clipped into perfect orbs. Forty years ago, they'd been shin-high shrubs threatened by every frost. She got out of the car and stood on the sidewalk.

"This isn't the right address," the driver said.

"I changed my mind," Amelia said. She let the car go and walked up the path to the front door—deep blue to match the shutters—and pushed the doorbell. The button was in exactly the same place on the doorframe and also sounded the same, a common ding-dong-dang that stabbed her with dismay. She had only used the doorbell if she'd mislaid her keys.

A woman in late middle age opened the door, her face youthful and open beneath a neat cap of gray hair. In New York, a woman as pretty as she would have colored her hair. Amelia's hair was dyed dark blond to match the color it had once been.

"Good afternoon, excuse me," she said. "I grew up in this house. You don't know me from Adam, but I thought I might be able to come in and look around." She laughed at the absurdity of her request.

"You must be Glenn's sister!" the woman said. "Glenn sold me this house when your mother passed. It's Amelia, right?"

"You know Glenn?" Amelia said.

"Oh, everybody knows Glenn," the woman said. "I'm so sorry about his heart attack. You're visiting him, of course." She opened the screen door wide to let Amelia pass through.

"I guess you'll find the place has changed a lot, but the bones are still the same. I'm Judy McBride."

Amelia stepped into a cone of pale light. *Beam me up, Scotty*, she thought as she looked up at a round frosted skylight.

"The hallway was so dark," Judy said. "It was a cinch to put that in."

"We used to keep a light on here even in the daytime." The lamp had sat on a table just inside the door, a knockoff Lladro figurine holding a shaded bulb like a torch. To the right off the hallway was a rectangular room that Amelia's mother had called the "parlor."

"I put in the sliding glass doors," Judy said as Amelia followed her in. "It's nice to be able to just walk out into the garden, and they open up the room, don't you think?"

Amelia and Glenn hadn't been allowed to go into this room when they were growing up. Reserved for guests who never arrived, parties never thrown, it had been a formal, chilly place that hadn't tempted her at all. Judy had painted the walls yellow and filled the room with comfortable furniture, a pillowy couch and two stuffed armchairs, all facing a brick fireplace that Amelia's parents had ignored. A newspaper lay open on the low coffee table next to an empty mug. Colorful abstract paintings hung on the walls.

"I'm an artist," Judy explained. "The paintings are mine."

"They're beautiful," Amelia said. "This room is brilliant. I don't even recognize it."

"No, it was rather gloomy. But that was the way our parents decorated, wasn't it? It was their idea of classy."

"Was it?" Amelia said. She hadn't thought of her parents aspiring to anything, though her mother had been hyperconscious of what people thought. She remembered being made to write thank-you notes for even a night spent at a friend's house, and both she and Glenn had been kept to a strict code of public manners. Any transgression was a reflection on her. An untucked shirt or an elbow on a table was enough to earn them her fury.

"You know, Glenn used to be an artist," she told Judy.

"Is that right?" Judy said. "He never said so. I wouldn't have guessed."

"In high school," Amelia said. "He was talented. He gave it up when he went to college." "Foolishness," their mother had called Glenn's gift for drawing. Their parents hadn't understood why a person would want to paint a picture when he could just go to Sears and buy one.

"Well, you must be curious to see the bedrooms," Judy said. "Which one was yours?"

"The one at the end of the hall. Glenn had the little one by the kitchen."

"But that's not really a bedroom," Judy said. "I use it as a pantry."

"The other bedroom was for guests," Amelia said. The "spare" room it had been called, another off-limits place. The only people who stayed in it were her mother's aunt, and, twice, an Army friend of her father's.

"Well, I use that one as my studio. I sleep in here, of course." Judy opened the door to the master bedroom. "I didn't do anything but give it a fresh coat of paint, though I thought about having a skylight in here as well."

Amelia's parents had slept in separate beds, and the window shades had always been drawn. The only decorations she could recall were a wooden crucifix on the wall between the beds and a china bowl on the chest of drawers that held safety pins and extra buttons. Her mother's strap had hung on a nail in the closet.

"I was afraid to go into this room when I was a kid," she said. "Our mother used to beat Glenn in here. She had a horrible temper; you never knew what would set her off. I could hear him screaming from every corner of the house." Unconsciously, she put her hands to her ears. "I would run out to the end of the road and hide in that little wooded patch between Dunston and Grant Avenue." She'd built a kind of hut with twigs and leaves that not even Glenn knew about. The roar of traffic from Grant feeding into the interstate had been a soothing sound: there were lots of other people in the world, people going home to peaceful homes, lives of grace and pleasure.

"Your mother?" Judy said. "Elaine? I'm surprised. We both went to the Church of St. Martin, so I saw her on Sundays. She seemed like a lovely woman."

"You don't believe me," Amelia said.

"Of course I do, if you say so. But I don't remember there being any woods between Dunston and Grant. A gated community has been there since I was a girl."

"It was torture growing up in this house," Amelia said.

Judy shifted from one foot to the other and crossed her arms over her chest. "Then why did you want to see it?"

"Honestly, I don't know," Amelia said. "I shouldn't have." She wished she'd stayed in New York, where nearly everything that happened earlier than last week was quickly erased by the present.

The bedroom's once-beige walls were lavender. Rose curtains hung at the two windows that faced the quiet street. It was a feminine room, serene and cozy. Amelia moved her gaze to the closet door. Her mother stood as still as a wax figure, holding the long brown strap in one hand. Her lips were so thin they were nearly invisible, her eyes narrow and filled with rage. She wore a pair of navy-blue slacks and a white cardigan with crystal buttons that Amelia recognized. She blinked. Her mother disappeared. *Oh, if only it had been as easy as that,* she thought. She turned and left the room.

In the car on the way back to Glenn's house, she made up her mind to return to New York that afternoon. She looked up the train schedule on her phone and checked her voicemail. She would find out if someone new was available tonight and uncork a bottle of wine.

"Trouble ahead," the driver said as they turned onto Glenn's street and pulled up behind an ambulance that was idling in front of the house.

"You have reached your destination," the GPS announced.

"Hang on," Amelia said to the driver. She watched the house, waiting to see what would come out the door, her temples booming like kettledrums. After a minute, Debbie's Beetle swerved down the street and parked askew on the opposite side of the ambulance. Debbie got out and stumbled up the steps, righted herself, and ran into the house. Amelia looked at the palms of her hands; they were glistening with sweat.

"Is this where you want to be or what?" the driver said.

"No, it's not," Amelia said. "But here I am anyway."

DOUBLE HAPPINESS

Gretchen didn't know anyone at Evan's party, and hadn't expected to, but she'd hoped she might meet some new people, fresh friends to enliven the dull winter. She searched for an amiable face in the crowd as she inched her way across the wide loft, encountering mouths and noses, necks and shoulders and backs, scents of perfume and stale breath. She hadn't been to Evan's place before and was startled by how large it was. They met on Tinder two weeks ago.

Her mother had once told her that a good way to start a conversation with a stranger was to ask him or her if they'd met before, so when she reached the bar table that had been set up by the kitchen, she blindly turned to the nearest body and said, "Hello, do I know you?"

"I don't know, do you?" said a ruddy-skinned man who wore a chartreuse silk vest and natty matching bow tie. Waiting for a drink on the opposite side of him was another guy whose fine-boned face had the silken quality of a Wedgewood figurine.

"Oh, maybe not," Gretchen said, raising her voice above the din. She tried to move toward the Wedgewood guy without being obvious about it.

"I'm Bob," the chartreuse man said. His eyes were small and watchful, the blue of the sea on a sunny day. She guessed he was in his late thirties. Older than she was, anyway.

"Gretchen," she said. She saw the Wedgewood guy pour himself a glass of wine and join two women near a potted ficus tree whose leaves were turning yellow. He too wore a tie, and the women wore dresses. Gretchen had one fancy outfit, a sequined sheath from a vintage store, but the sequins were falling off in sparkling strands, and she hadn't been able to reattach them. The combat boots and artfully torn leggings she'd chosen to wear tonight made her feel like a disaffected teenager.

"What can I get you?" Bob said.

Someone else to talk to, she thought. "Just a beer, no glass. I'm Evan's girlfriend, by the way."

"Ah." He studied her. She wondered what he thought he saw. "How long have you two been an item?"

"A while," she said as she accepted the beer.

"What's 'a while'?" he said.

"'A while' is an amount of time."

He laughed, exposing an overbite. "You're a cheeky one, aren't you?"

Gretchen looked at him for a beat before saying, "I'm not anything, as far as you're concerned. You don't know me at all."

He raised his hands in surrender. "I've been told I'm an ass."

"And do you think you are?" she said.

"Yes, probably." He glanced over her head. "I could tell you wished you were talking to that handsome guy who just walked away. I know him, I could introduce you, if you'd like. He's married, but that wouldn't matter to you, since you're involved with Evan."

For a second, Gretchen was speechless. She was pinned where she stood by a woman on one side of her and a man on the other, both waiting to get a drink at the bar. "Touché," she said. "So how do you know Evan?"

"We're brothers."

"Really? You look nothing alike."

Bob reached out and caught the arm of a passing woman whose red lipstick bled beyond the boundaries of her mouth. She looked at him as if without recognition before bestowing a slow smile. "This young lady doesn't believe I'm Evan's brother."

"Who else would you be?" she said and was carried away on the current of the crowd.

"Why hasn't Evan ever mentioned you?" Gretchen said.

"You'd have to ask him that," Bob said.

"Well, I would, but I can't find him in this mob."

Rather than looking around for Evan, he kept his eyes fixed on her. "He might not be here."

"Of course he is, this is his party."

Bob shrugged. "Am I my brother's keeper?"

All of a sudden she felt defeated. The party's chaotic atmosphere had developed a sinister edge in her mind, as if a violence of some kind was bound to happen, irrevocable and dire. Evan had told her the party would be casual and small, with only close friends invited. Why had he lied? He'd made her look like a fool. She wouldn't call him again. If he called her, she wouldn't pick up. Their relationship didn't amount to much. They'd only slept together three times, but she thought she had a right to be angry. "I'm leaving now," she said.

"Good idea," Bob said. "I know a bar that's a lot of fun. We could go there."

How did I *become* we? she thought. "What's so fun about it?"

"It's called Double Happiness, in Chinatown—do you know it? It looks like it's been dug out of a cave, and they have a flaming drink called a Dragon's Breath. They serve dumplings and things, too, if you're hungry." He gave her a sidelong glance. "My treat."

Gretchen was in fact very hungry, but only had six

dollars, thirty-two cents, and a maxed-out credit card in her wallet. She barely made ends meet as a freelance graphic designer, a career she'd come to New York to pursue, starting as a lowly assistant at a design firm and eventually going out on her own. She was failing at it in increments. Fewer jobs came her way every year. But she had become so bored with the work that it didn't matter to her anymore. "Sure, why not," she said.

"Fantastic!" Bob tucked his arm into hers. She hesitated, scanning the crowd one more time. "I won't tell Evan," he said. "We hardly ever talk anyway."

"Maybe that's why he never mentioned you," she said. But she hadn't told Evan anything about her family either. So far, all they'd done was meet for a quick drink somewhere and go back to her place for sex.

"He and I don't get along very well," Bob said. He made a ridiculous boohoo face.

She almost accused him of using her just to piss off his brother, but so what if he was? Double Happiness awaited.

The taxicab stopped beside a waist-high berm of gray snow pocked with yellow melts of pee. Gretchen climbed over the snow like a goat, holding her arms out for balance; Bob got out of the cab on the opposite side and made a careful detour through a clear space in the curb. He took them down an iron stairwell to an unmarked door where the odor of urine combined with disinfectant cleaner was nearly overpowering.

The place was lit only by glowing candles. The walls appeared to be made of rocks and the ceiling was a low, mud-colored dome. Several small tables and mismatched chairs surrounded a long chrome bar. A number of alcoves, obscured by bead curtains, appeared to have been gouged out of the facing wall. A tall Chinese man wearing a tuxedo led them to an alcove with a red, soda fountain–style booth that looked like a relic from the fifties. Drawings and initials and random words were carved into the Formica surface of the table. From a speaker above the bar came a woman's voice singing a twanging, plaintive song.

Bob murmured something to the man, who nodded and disappeared. There seemed to be no one else in the place. Maybe it was an after-hours spot. It was only half past nine.

She reached out and touched the wall. It really was made of rock. "How do you know this place is called Double Happiness if there's no sign outside?"

"I know because a friend said so," Bob said as he shucked his wool overcoat. "It's a phenomenon known as word of mouth." He gave her a bright look. "So. Here we are. Tell me everything."

"Everything about what?" she said.

"About yourself!" he said. "Let's start with where you're from."

"Here," she said. "New York."

"No, you're not."

"How can you tell?"

"You have a Midwestern accent, for one thing, and you don't look like a New Yorker. There's something wide-eyed about you."

"I'm not wide-eyed. I'm almost thirty."

"No, that kind of look never goes away, even when you're old and jaded."

"Okay, I'm from Cleveland, but I've been living in the East a long time. I went to art school in Philadelphia."

"But you're not an artist, are you?" he said with a certainty she found annoying.

"I am too. Sort of." She told him what she did for a living.

"Sounds as if you hate it," he said.

"What I hate are clients who don't know what they

want," she said. "I show them designs and they don't like any of them, but they can't ever tell me what they do want. It's infuriating."

"Most people don't know what they want."

"I know what I want."

"Oh yes? What do you want?"

She traced the marks on the table with her finger. "To be happy."

"That's too generic. Everyone wants to be happy, or so they say. What, specifically, do you want?"

She searched the inventory stacked up in her mind. "I want a leather jacket I saw in a boutique in the Village."

He shook his head. "Objects don't count, particularly clothes. I'm talking about things like wanting to be a doctor, or wanting to live abroad, wanting to build a house with your own hands."

"Build a house with your own hands?"

"I had an uncle who talked about doing that. Sadly, he never did."

"So, what do you want?" she said.

"I'm not going to tell you until you tell me."

She regarded him through narrowed eyes. "Maybe it's none of your business."

"Meaning you don't know," he said. "I have a friend who tells fortunes. She's scarily accurate. You don't have to know what you want; she tells you what you'll get."

The bead curtain parted with a muted clatter. The Chinese man put a wide-bowled, long-stemmed glass on the table and produced a sparkler from his breast pocket. He lit the sparkler and touched it to the pink liquid in the glass. The surface of the liquid flickered yellow before the flame gathered momentum and flared. Even as she leaned away, Gretchen could feel its warmth.

The flame died as quickly as it had come to life. The man handed them long plastic straws and disappeared once more.

Gretchen dipped her straw into the drink. It tasted like raspberries and lemonade.

"Oh, it's cold! I didn't expect that. Delicious, what's in it?"

"Cointreau? Vermouth? Lighter fluid?" Bob said. "Some things should remain a mystery."

Again, the bead curtain parted. The man put a bamboo dumpling steamer on the table and gave them each a small bowl of noodles. Hungrily, Gretchen dug in with a pair of chopsticks, holding the bowl up to her chin to avoid losing a single noodle before it reached her mouth. Bob toyed with his food, sucking up noodles one by one. When Gretchen's bowl was empty, she took a draw of the Dragon's Breath. She smiled at Bob. "Good stuff. Packs a punch."

"I knew you'd like it here," he said. "Not everybody does."

"No, I can imagine, it's not exactly the Plaza. Anyway, we just met, so how could you have known what I'd like?" She was hoping he'd say something complimentary. She couldn't remember the last compliment she'd received. She wanted to be told she was special in some way by a man other than her father, who had believed since her birth that she would conquer the world and refused against all evidence to be convinced otherwise. Bob asked her questions, at least. Most men only wanted to talk about themselves. She checked her phone. There were three texts from Evan: *where r u, where r u,* and an angry face emoji. The first text had come in an hour and a half ago, the emoji in the past three minutes. *Oh, fuck off,* she thought as she put the phone back in her purse.

The man brought another Dragon's Breath just as Bob finished the dregs of the first one. Again, the flame whooshed up.

"It's less exciting the second time," Bob said. "But the third time is absolutely thrilling."

Gretchen felt the familiar elation, bright and crisp, that

preceded the slide into drunkenness. She took the lid off the steamer and maneuvered her chopsticks around a dumpling. "I like you," she said. "You're nothing like Evan."

"You didn't like me at first," Bob said.

"I can't remember if I did or not. That was a long time ago."

Bob checked his watch, a thin gold disk fastened by an alligator band. "Oh yes, ages ago. But the night is still young. What shall we do next?"

She took a long sip and left a swallow in the glass. "I'm not sleeping with you."

"No, of course not. I wouldn't presume. I have a girl-friend, anyway. Anemone Villeneuve. She lives in Far Rock-away, in a house on the beach. She's visiting her aunt in St. Lucia for the week, or she would be sitting where you are right now."

"I don't believe a word of what you just said. Anemone Villeneuve. What a preposterous name."

"Jean Smith, then."

"Too plain. How about Maya? I've always liked that name."

"Maya Fiorello," he said. "Italian on her father's side, Mexican on her mother's."

"She sounds nice," Gretchen said. "I hope you'll be very happy."

"Hey, there's a stand of Citi Bikes a block away," he said. "Let's get a couple of them and ride over to my friend's, have our fortunes told."

"It's like two degrees outside," she said.

"Oh, don't be a sissy," he said.

"Okay, but can we have another Dragon's Breath first?"

As if he'd heard her, the man reappeared.

"Woo hoo!" Gretchen said as the drink flickered, then flared.

She hadn't ridden a bike since she was a teenager and felt wobbly on it at first, but after a couple of blocks she found her bearings and cruised along behind Bob through the deserted streets of the Lower East Side. Metal shutters had been pulled down over the shops, though the windows of the apartments above them were bright. She had lived in New York for almost eight years, yet she was unfamiliar with this part of town. They passed fabric stores and lighting wholesalers, a small museum devoted to the history of tenements; every now and then she caught sight of a bridge, either the Williamsburg or Manhattan, she didn't know which. The streetlights seemed dimmer than they were uptown, the darkness between them deeper. A rat scurried in front of her bike, so big she mistook it for a cat.

"I'm freezing!" she shouted.

"I know!" Bob said. "Isn't it great?" He took his hands off the handlebars and crossed his arms over his chest. The end of his scarf fluttered over his shoulder. He looked like a boy showing off. Then he grabbed the handlebars again and pedaled standing up. Gretchen breathed heavily as she tried to keep pace, sweating inside her parka. Finally, he pulled up in front of a narrow brownstone and took his phone out of his coat pocket. "It's me!" he said in a delighted voice. "Yes, right downstairs."

A window three flights up slid open. "Hiya!" said the silhouette of a woman's head as a tin can on a string descended. Bob caught the can and fished out a key. Gretchen followed him up a flight of steps and waited for him to open the building's door. The foyer was lit by a flickering fluorescent tube, but the stairway was almost too dim to see. She hung on to the banister, watching her step. The key in the tin can business had seemed like something out of an old movie. She lived in a building where you buzzed people in.

"Maybe I'll go," she said. She turned around but was

afraid to walk down alone.

"No!" Bob said. "This is the best part."

"The best part of what?" she said.

A woman leaned over the banister above them. When they reached the landing, Bob said, "Elaine, meet Gretchen. Gretchen, Elaine. Elaine is one of my oldest friends." Elaine was very fat. Her flossy platinum hair framed her face like a cloud. She wore an orange terry cloth bathrobe and a pair of cheap terry scuffs.

"Welcome," she said with a regal sweep of her hand. Coming in from the dark landing, Gretchen squinted against the yellow light cast by a globe-shaped ceiling fixture. The furniture, what little there was, looked as if each piece had originated from a different house. "You sit there," Elaine told her, indicating a red leather ottoman. "You," she pointed at Bob, "can sit anywhere you like." She waddled over to a kitchenette, humming to herself. She returned a minute later with a demitasse of coffee held on the flat of her hand. She offered the coffee to Gretchen. Puzzled, Gretchen took a sip. The cup was only half-full, and the coffee was lukewarm and bitter. Elaine took the cup from her and turned it over onto a handkerchief in a saucer. The remainder of the coffee seeped through the fibers of the white fabric, staining it brown to its edges. She sat down on a filthy chintz-covered chair, turned the cup upright, and peered inside it.

"What are you doing?" Gretchen said.

"I'm studying your grounds," Elaine said. "Isn't that why you're here?"

Bob stood at the window, spying on the people in the apartment across the street. He turned and said, "Elaine is a psychic, I told you that. She reads coffee grounds."

"I've never met a psychic," Gretchen said. "How do I know you're real?"

"I'm sitting here in front of you," Elaine said with a laugh. "How much more real do you want?"

"I mean a real psychic," Gretchen said.

"That you can't know," Elaine said. She gazed inside the cup.

Gretchen was fascinated by Elaine's lack of vanity, the way she sat like a Sumo wrestler with her gigantic legs spread, the crotch of her white underpants displayed. There was a full-length mirror on the wall by the door. Did she check her reflection before she went out? How much would a person have to eat to get so fat?

"Ah hah," Elaine said. "I see a man with a mustache. He's all right, but you've had a misunderstanding. A missed connection. He likes you more than you think." Gretchen frowned. Evan had a mustache, but so did a lot of men. "You won't be here much longer," Elaine went on. "I'd say less than a year."

Gretchen gasped. "Why? What's wrong with me?"

Elaine looked up. "Nothing's wrong with you. I mean you won't be in New York much longer."

"Where will I be?"

"Somewhere you've lived before."

"I don't believe you," Gretchen said.

"Suit yourself," Elaine said. "So, the mustache guy. You've misjudged him. No, not him, exactly, but something around him."

"Why do you keep talking about him?" Gretchen said.

"I don't know," Elaine said. "I'm only reading what I see. Home! You'll be going home."

"No way," Gretchen said.

Elaine looked at Bob. "You've brought me a doubter."

Gretchen felt her face go hot. In her mind's eye she saw her mother doing laundry in the laundry nook at home—efficiently separating the lights from the darks, measuring out fabric softener—then saw herself dragging a bag of dirty clothes down to her building's basement laundry room only to find that the machines were out of order, or she didn't have the right change, or she'd forgotten the detergent. She could easily get work in Cleveland. She'd have the élan of coming from New York. Whenever she went home for a visit, her high school friends treated her like a celebrity.

"I don't know what I want," she wailed. "I used to know, but it didn't work out. Why doesn't anything fucking work out?" She had at one time imagined herself as the owner of a successful design studio. She would have worn dramatic eye makeup and mannish black clothes and had a "partner" rather than a husband, because being married would have been one of the many conventions she would have thrown off like an unfashionable coat. Her fantasy even extended to what breed of dog she would have: an Italian greyhound, delicate and sleek, outfitted with a silver collar. She wiped her nose with the back of her hand. "Evan has a mustache. Do you think I'm meant to be with him?"

"Hard to say," Elaine said. "It might be too late."

Bob sat on the couch and rested his elbows on his knees. His dun hair had been flattened against his head by his cap. "Gretchen, listen to me. Evan wasn't at the party tonight because he didn't give the party. It was given by a friend of mine."

"But why would Evan say it was his party?" Gretchen said.

"He didn't," Bob said. "You went to the wrong party."

Gretchen attempted to absorb this. "That sounds like a riddle. But where is Evan?"

"Presumably at his place, wondering where you are," Bob said. "Give me your phone. Do you have his address in there?"

"Why would you need his address?" Gretchen said as she handed over her phone. "I don't understand at all."

"Here it is," Bob said after scrolling through her contacts. "The party you went to was at 420 West Broadway. Evan's address is 420 East Broadway."

"Fourth floor," Gretchen said.

"Yes," Bob said. "But the wrong address. Do you understand what I'm saying? Why don't we go there now?"

"What are the odds of that happening?" Elaine said. "What are you up to, Bob? This poor girl is too drunk for your shenanigans."

"But you and Evan don't get along," Gretchen said. "I don't want to be involved."

Bob bit his lip. Elaine examined her fingernails, which were a rich vermillion and unusually long.

"Gretchen, I'm not really Evan's brother. I only said I was, I don't know why. It seemed funny at the time. I've never met the guy."

"Ha ha, sure," Gretchen said. She looked at Elaine. "No, wait, seriously?"

Bob took her hand and pulled her to her feet. "Thanks, Elaine," he said.

Elaine heaved herself out of her chair. "Yeah, okay. Bring someone sober next time."

Leaving the Citi Bikes in Elaine's foyer, Bob hailed a cab on Delancey, where the traffic whizzed back and forth on two lanes. "Call Evan," he said, handing Gretchen her phone.

"I think I need to throw up," she said.

Bob rolled down her window. "Do it out there, if you have to," he said. "But for God's sake, keep quiet or the cabby will kick us out." He took her phone and tapped Evan's number, then handed the phone back to her.

She frowned. "Says the voice mailbox is full."

"Fine, we're almost there anyway."

"Why does this cab smell like bubble gum?" she said. "Hey, do you like me, Bob? Can we be an item?" She leaned into him and put her head on his shoulder.

"Why not," he said in tired voice. "But let's find Evan

first. Right here is fine," he told the driver. "You can leave us at the corner." He handed the driver a twenty and hustled Gretchen out of the car.

"But if we're an item, I don't need Evan," she said. "I don't care about him anymore."

"Then you should tell him that," Bob said. He took her arm and began walking. The street was dark and deserted except for a café at the end of the block. Far beyond, the lights of uptown cast a halo in the sky. "I'm sorry, I shouldn't have lied to you."

"Why did you?" Gretchen said.

"Because I'm an ass," he said. "I told you that."

"Listen, why haven't you said anything nice to me? You haven't said one nice thing." She stumbled on a break in the sidewalk. "Stop, you're going too fast."

He stopped. "What nice thing do you want to hear?"

Every nice thing, she thought. An avalanche of compliments. "Obviously if I tell you it doesn't count."

After a moment's thought, he said, "You're a good sport."

"Are you kidding me? You can lie your head off about everything but you can't bring yourself to give me a better compliment than that? I don't think you're so great either."

She pushed his gloved hand off her arm and walked away without him. The neighborhood was far from her own. She figured she'd recognize something eventually, a street or a building: a landmark.

LOVE IS NOT ENOUGH

My sister's boyfriend's name was Robin, which struck me as a girlish name for a guy, but he was as big as a yeti and had a forest of dark hair on his arms. When she brought him home to Connecticut to meet our mother and me, he seemed to dwarf the house: he was a grown-up, fully a man, and Jeannie was obviously besotted. She was twenty-two, a year out of college; he was in his thirties. He sat on the love-seat in the living room holding Jeannie's comparatively tiny hand and talked for a long time. Then they got up and went out to dinner somewhere in Darien, or maybe they drove back to the city. I stared at the depression in the sofa where he'd sat and tried to remember what he'd said, but mostly recalled the flashes of his too-white teeth, and the bluish tint of his five o'clock shadow. I'd felt shy around him for a reason I couldn't have named.

"He's handsome, I'll give him that," my mother said after they left. "But that's all I'll give him. Jeannie is too easy, always has been. She'd go out with the mailman if he asked her."

It was six o'clock on the dot and she was pouring herself a glass of vodka, the only type of alcohol her latest diet allowed. I had to take Jeannie's word for it that our mother had once been kind. When I was five, and Jeannie was fifteen, our father went into the woods in back of our house and shot himself in the head. According to Jeannie, our mother had been a different person before then. I took that literally for a long time, imagining a woman I'd never met, but when I finally understood, I felt sorry for her and blamed her a little bit less for the way she was now.

First thing the next morning, Jeannie called.

"So what do you think?" she said. "He's amazing, isn't he?"

"Amazing," I said. For all I knew, Robin was amazing. I didn't want to be disagreeable.

"He was impressed by you, Katie," she said.

"By me? Why?"

"He thinks you're very mature for your age."

"I hardly said anything." In fact, I hadn't said anything at all. I seemed older than twelve because I was tall and quiet. I knew that some people thought the reason for my maturity was the circumstances of my father's death. I didn't know anyone who hadn't heard how he died, because my mother had told, and continued to tell, everyone connected to us. Jeannie also talked openly about it and had certainly told Robin by now.

"I'm in love," she said. "This is it. He's the one."

"How can you tell?"

"I can tell because I think about him all the time. I can't wait to see him, and when I'm with him I feel so turned on I can hardly stand it." She lowered her voice. "He's great in bed."

Jeannie had been telling me about her sex life since she began to have one at the age of seventeen. I was her confidante, her audience, even in the days when I didn't understand a word of what she said. When she'd had an abortion a year ago, she'd told me about that too. "I know, I know, I know," I'd kept saying as she described the procedure in detail, hoping she'd skip ahead to the end. Finally she'd said, "Stop saying you know! You don't know anything about it!" *I know all about it now,* I'd thought, vowing to never have one myself.

"Does he think you're the one too?" I was stretched out on my bed with my head propped on a stuffed elephant. I had about twenty plush animals arranged against the head-board. When I was younger, I imagined they came to life the minute I walked out of my room.

"He has to say he loves me before I say it to him," Jeannie said.

"How come?"

"I don't want to say it and have him not say it back—that would be humiliating."

"He seemed to like you a lot," I said. "He held your hand the whole time he was here." I had only just begun to think about boys as anything but obnoxious, but I knew from watching the kids in the grade ahead of mine that holding hands was a sign of commitment.

"What does Mom think? I bet she said he's too old for me."

Our mother had called Robin "common" and "slick" after she'd had a few drinks. I'd stuck up for him because Jeannie liked him.

"Oh, and you're such an expert on men," she'd said, her face ruddy and her eyes belligerent. *How much do you know about them?* I'd wanted to say, because she had never in my memory been on one date. She'd been sitting in the same upholstered chair she sat in every night. The nubbly cream fabric behind her head was stained yellow from the many times she'd passed out and slept there for hours.

"Mom said he's handsome," I said. I could hear Jeannie breathe a short huff of relief. But she was right to assume our mother thought Robin was too old.

"How has she been lately?"

"The same," I said.

"Drinking a lot?"

"Yeah."

"Is she being nice to you?"

"Not really." She had screamed at me a few days before for not arranging the dishes properly in the dishwasher. I never knew what would set her off; the dishes had looked fine to me. She'd been drunk at the time, but she didn't have to be to fly into one of her rages.

"Listen, why don't you take the train into the city next weekend? We can go shopping, get you some clothes before school starts. I'll take Saturday off from the store."

Visiting Jeannie was my favorite thing to do. She had a studio apartment in the East Village that was just large enough to accommodate a twin bed that she made into a sofa during the day. I slept in a sleeping bag on the floor. Sometimes we got cheap tickets from TKTS and went to a Broadway musical, though usually we went to the movies, or watched TV and shared an order of my favorite meal, sesame chicken and spring rolls. Jeannie had a wonderful, offbeat taste in clothing and found all sorts of things at vintage stores. Shopping with her was a treat, as unlike trudging around Nordstrom with our mother as New York was unlike Darien.

When I got off the train at Grand Central early Friday evening, Jeannie wasn't under the clock. People walked around me from every direction as I stood in confusion, a rock in a confluence of rivers. She was always under the clock. She would be there in a minute, I thought. Five minutes turned to fifteen, fifteen to twenty. When I took out my phone to call her, she appeared before me as if she'd been standing there all along.

"Were you scared?" she said. "I'm sorry. I got hung up." She was wearing a silvery lace slip under a sheer black dress whose neckline plunged to her waist. Dangling from her ears was a pair of crescent-shaped gold earrings that had three red beads in the shape of tears suspended from their lower edges. Her blond hair was piled on top of her head, tendrils falling down around her neck. She looked beautiful and not like herself.

"Why are you dressed up?" I said. She looked down at her clothes as if she'd forgotten what she was wearing.

"Big surprise," she said. "We're going to the theater!"

"Oh, wow! What show?"

"It's not a musical, it's a play," she said. "And we're going out to an early dinner first." She picked up my overnight bag and started walking the wrong way.

"Wait," I said, pointing in the opposite direction. "Aren't we taking the subway to your apartment?" We always took the six train to Astor Place and walked to Second Avenue.

"No, we're not staying there tonight, we're staying at Robin's. We're meeting him at the restaurant, there's a car waiting outside. Come on," she said, and grabbed my hand. We ran up the huge marble staircase to Vanderbilt Avenue, where a black sedan idled at the curb. Its back seat smelled like leather and there was wood paneling inside the doors. The driver pulled away from the curb without being told where to go.

"The restaurant we're going to is really nice," Jeanie said.

"But I'm wearing shorts," I said. They were cutoffs from a pair of last year's jeans.

"That's okay. It doesn't matter what you're wearing." She leaned forward and adjusted the air conditioning vent. I had on a tank top, and my arms were covered with goose bumps. I longed to join the hot, noisy city that paraded past the car windows.

"You're all dressed up. Shouldn't I be?"

"You're twelve, Katie. Nobody cares how you look."

Her patronizing tone made me mad. "Nobody cares how you look, either."

She laughed at me. "Robin does! He bought me these earrings; do you like them? Come on, Katie, this is going to be so fun."

"Okay," I said. I wanted to please her. I had forgotten about Robin. She had never included a boyfriend on any of my other visits, but the difference now was she was in love.

"Were you ever in love before?" I said.

She looked out the window. "No. I could never take anyone seriously. The guys I used to go out with were children compared to Robin."

"He's rich, isn't he?" I said. The car, the restaurant, the earrings. I had never ridden in even a regular taxicab with Jeannie, and take-out food was a treat. The careful way she touched the earrings made me think they were expensive.

"He makes a good living," she said with a hint of pride in her voice.

"Why are we staying with him?" I said.

"It's much more comfortable at his place. He's got an extra room for one thing. You won't have to sleep on the floor."

"I like your place. I don't mind sleeping on the floor."

"You'll like this better," she said.

The restaurant was called La Grande Idée. The Big Idea. I knew that because I took French at school. We were led by a tuxedoed maître d' through a roomful of tables covered with spotless white cloths. On each was an arrangement of fresh summer flowers; I lingered behind Jeannie to admire them and thought of the patchy perennial border at home that our mother sometimes dug around in. There were only two other diners, an elderly couple. It was as cold here as it had been in the car, and bright with long rays of evening sun. I tugged at the back of my shorts, conscious of my skimpy clothes, but Jeannie was right: nobody noticed what I was wearing. The maître d' seated us next to a window with a view of a profusely green Central Park. He shook out our napkins and placed them on our laps and handed a folded piece of notepaper to Jeannie.

"Robin says he'll be late, to start without him," she said as she read the note. I wondered why he hadn't simply texted or phoned, but Jeannie's smile as she unfolded the paper made me think that receiving a note from your boyfriend was romantic, like a boy passing a note in school.

"How did you meet him?" I said after we'd ordered. I thought I should have already known how they met; it would have been explained when Jeannie brought him home. I didn't remember either my mother or myself asking a single question, though my mother must have asked a few at least. For her not to wouldn't have made sense.

"We met at the store," Jeannie said. "He came in and bought a set of towels, and we ended up talking for an hour. My manager went ballistic after he left."

"Who went ballistic?" Robin sat down between us. He took Jeannie's hand and kissed it. I recognized the romance in that. He wore a dark blue suit and a red-and-blue striped tie; strangely, the starched collar of his shirt was white while the rest of it was pale blue. He turned to me and said, "Katie, how are you?" as if he honestly wanted to know. I wasn't used to people being interested in me.

"Fine, thank you," I said.

"Hot out, isn't it? Hotter than it was in Connecticut, I bet. What's your favorite season?"

"Summer," I said.

"Summer! Of course! No school. Summer is my favorite, too." Even though he seemed completely focused on me, his hand was on Jeannie's arm. I looked at her. Her cheeks were pink. I thought she looked a little hectic, but her dress was interesting. Had Robin bought that, too?

"Doesn't your sister look lovely?" he said.

"She looks different than usual. But she's always pretty."

"She is." He gazed at her. Romantic moment number

three. I sat in the pooling silence, intent on extracting an orange flower from my miniscule green salad.

"Did Jeannie tell you we're going to a play?" he said. "It's a very famous one. It's called *Waiting for Godot.*"

The name of the play meant nothing to me, but I smiled and nodded as if it did. I wanted to make a good impression because of Jeannie being in love with him, and because I was conscious of the fact that he thought I was mature. He ordered a drink called a gimlet, drank it quickly, and ordered another one right away. He seemed like anyone now, a pleasant guy. I couldn't imagine why he'd struck me speechless before.

"Aren't you going to eat anything?" I said.

He looked at his watch. "Too early, I think. You go ahead. I'll get something after the play. You two look alike, you know that? Same eyes? No, not the eyes. Same . . . something. I can't put my finger on it."

No one had ever said Jeannie and I looked alike. I was a brunette and she was fair, and we were ten years apart in age.

"You think so?" Jeannie said. She winked at me. I had no idea what the wink meant. She had never winked at me in my life. I wanted to go back to Grand Central and find my real sister under the clock.

The play was boring in every possible way. There was no set, only a bare stage with a flimsy, leafless tree; the two actors' costumes were identically dust-colored and ratty, as if they'd been wearing them for years. I was used to the lavish costumes and set designs of popular musicals, to simple plots and catchy songs that were easily followed and remembered. But I couldn't find even the skeleton of a plot in the yammering back-and-forth dialogue. I must have sighed or made an impatient movement, because Jeannie leaned into me.

"They're waiting for a guy named Godot to show up," she whispered. I had gathered that much already.

"When is he coming?" I said.

She turned to Robin and conferred with him, then came back to me with a dismayed look on her face. "Robin says never."

"You're kidding," I said. I couldn't believe it.

A woman behind us made a shushing noise, so Jeannie settled back into her seat. I felt the solid weight of boredom descend on me. The actors talked on and on, sitting against the tree. When one of them suggested they hang themselves, I fervently hoped they would. Because of my father, suicide wasn't shocking to me. He'd been in the woods when he shot himself. He might have sat against a tree. It had been February, so the trees would have been bare, but if there had been snow on the ground, he wouldn't have wanted to sit down. It would have been bleak in the bare, cold woods. Jeannie once told me he had been in a state of despair, though she didn't know why. I thought that he might have chosen the woods because it looked the way he felt. All of a sudden, I wanted to know what he'd been thinking about when he pulled the trigger.

"I have to go to the bathroom," I whispered to Jeannie, and left my seat before she could reply. I crabbed my way across the long row, brushing people's knees with my shins, and ran up the aisle past a uniformed usher toward a lighted sign for the ladies' room. Inside, the walls were unremittingly pink, and there was a long marble counter of sinks. I patted my face with a handful of tepid water and dried it with an unusually thick paper towel. I went into a stall and Googled my father's name. I was surprised by how many people had the same name, so I added my mother's name and the name of our town. There was a brief obituary in the *Stamford Advocate*:

> *Stanley Parsons died suddenly on February 18th at the age of 42. Born and raised in Stamford, Connecticut, he resided in Darien. He leaves behind his beloved wife, Sharon, and cherished daughters Jean and Katherine. Services are private. In lieu of flowers, donations may be made to the Nature Conservancy of Connecticut.*

I sat down on the toilet. That he'd been a nature lover made me change my mind about why he'd gone into the woods. Maybe he'd looked up at the tops of the trees, at a flock of birds in a cloudless sky; maybe he'd listened to the wind rustle the dry leaves on the ground or turned his face toward the weak winter sun. I imagined him taking a last look around at the world before putting the gun to his head.

I sat there for a while, crying noiselessly into my hands. I'd never cried about him before and felt like a phony crying now. I remembered he'd smoked cigarettes and had a big, raucous laugh. I didn't see how it was possible to have a laugh like that and be in a state of despair. I blew my nose on a clutch of toilet paper just as a group of people came in. Stall doors banged shut.

"Katie?" Jeannie called. "Are you in here, Katie?"

"Here," I said. I unlocked the stall door. She opened it and came in.

"I'm sorry about the play," she said. "I didn't know how dull it would be. Robin thinks it's deep, but I don't get it at all." She looked at my phone. "Are you on Snapchat or something?" I turned the phone around so she could see the screen. She frowned. "Oh, Katie, no. Why are you looking at that?"

"Is it true that he cherished us?"

She leaned against the pink metal door. "Of course."

"I think that's just what people say in obituaries. 'Beloved,' 'cherished.' Who knows how he felt."

Jeannie only sighed. I had expected her to stick up for him; she had known him, after all. "What's this about?" she said. "Why are you thinking about him now?"

"Did he leave a note?" I said. I surprised myself with the question. I'd never wondered if he'd left a note before, but now that I'd asked, I felt certain he had.

She crossed her arms and looked at the floor. "Yes. A short one."

"What did it say?"

"It said, 'Love is not enough.' I didn't see it, but that's what I was told."

"What does it mean?"

"It means that even the love of his family wasn't enough to keep him from wanting to die."

"That's terrible," I said.

"I wish I hadn't told you. You weren't supposed to know. Now you'll be emotionally scarred, and it'll be my fault."

"I won't be scarred," I said.

"Don't tell Mom I told you." She gave me her hand and pulled me up. "Come on, it's intermission. Let's get a Coke."

We went to another restaurant after the play because Robin wanted something to eat. It was a different kind of restaurant than La Grande Idée, very busy and not as fancy, with high ceilings and paper tablecloths and brisk waiters who wore white aprons. Robin drank a gimlet, then ordered another, as well as a steak and a bottle of wine. Even though we'd eaten before, I ordered a bowl of chocolate ice cream, and Jeannie had a Caesar salad. When the food came, Robin poured me a glass of wine. I thought he was being funny.

"Go ahead," he said. "Try it."

"Robin," Jeannie said. "She's twelve." She took the glass and put it by her plate. Robin put it back beside mine.

"Let her have a sip," he said.

"What if she doesn't want one?"

"I don't," I said. "But thank you."

"But thank you," he mimicked in a high, mincing voice.

I froze as if his eyes were searchlights. He'd had too much to drink. When my mother was drunk, I avoided trouble by doing exactly what she told me to do. The wine was so dark it was almost black; it looked like an evil potion. I reached for the glass and took a sip. It tasted bitter and felt dry on my tongue.

"What did you think of the play?" he said. "Boring? It's about boredom, actually. Boredom as existential confinement."

"Right," I said, as if I understood. It was important to agree with everything a drunk person said.

"Katie gets it," he said to Jeannie. "I guess little sister got the brains in the family." He knocked his head with his fist. "Pretty, but not so bright, your big sister."

I looked at Jeannie. She was eating her salad. The restaurant was noisy; I told myself she hadn't heard him. "Jeannie is the smartest person I know," I said. I couldn't help myself.

"Oh yeah?" He took a bite of his steak and spoke with a full mouth. "How many people over the age of twelve do you know?"

"Lots," I said. "And she's the nicest person, too."

Jeannie stood up. "I'll be right back." She was gone before I could ask to come with her. I got up anyway to follow her, but Robin grabbed my hand.

"Sit," he said. He pointed at the wine glass with his fork. "I dare you to drink it all."

"Why?" I said.

He leaned in so close I could see the pores on his nose. He smelled like my mother when she was drunk. "Double-dare you," he said.

I held my breath and drank half the wine in the glass. "You're like my mom," I said, then held my breath again and finished the rest. *So there, you jerk,* I thought. "She gets drunk and mean, too."

"Is that so?" Robin said. "Your father committed suicide and your mother is a drunk. Nice family. No wonder Jeannie's such a mess."

"She's not a mess!" I said. "You're lucky she lets you date her."

"Oh, am I?" His laugh was harsh, a cough. "You think you're cute, don't you? I'll bet you do. In your short-shorts with your ass hanging out, those itty-bitty tits under that tight little top." As he waved his hand dismissively, he almost touched my breasts. I wondered if he would be embarrassed when he remembered this moment tomorrow. He leaned toward me and said, "You're ordinary, nothing special about you. You'll never have an iota of Jeannie's sex appeal. Jeannie is a hell of a lay." He sat back again and stared past me, his jaw working as if he were chewing.

Why are you telling me this? I wanted to ask. I was more puzzled than offended. Hearing a man speak of my "ass" and "tits" gave me the creepiest feeling I'd ever had. I looked around, searching for Jeannie. My eyes felt too large for their sockets. I saw her walking toward me from the far end of the room as if through a periscope.

"We missed you," Robin said as she reached the table and sat down.

"Katie, I hope you didn't drink that whole glass of wine," she said.

"She did," Robin said. "Downed it like a Bowery bum."

"He made me," I said.

"I made you?" he said in false astonishment. "What, did I force it down your gullet?"

Jeannie looked from Robin to me. "Eat your ice cream," she said. My ice cream was a brown puddle by this time. I obediently spooned it into my mouth.

"Your sister was just telling me that your mother has a

problem with alcohol," Robin said. Jeannie stared at me with a horrified expression, her glazed pink lips slack with surprise. We never talked about our mother to anyone but each other; it was an unspoken pact we'd kept for as long as I could remember. Jeannie would yell at me later for being a traitor to our mother and embarrassing us. But I thought our father's death was equally embarrassing. I knew that Jeannie and our mother talked about it to set themselves apart from regular people. Sometimes they even seemed proud. I wanted the opposite, to be like everyone else. I had no memory of being a kid whose family was unremarkable.

"I feel sick," I said. I stood up too quickly and almost fell. Jeannie caught me by the elbow. She led me across the restaurant and down a narrow flight of stairs. I banged through the door to the ladies' room and rushed into a stall. It felt like everything I'd eaten in my whole life came roaring out of my mouth. Jeannie stood over me, holding my hair. When I was done, she took me to the sink and made me wash out my mouth with water from the tap. The walls of the bathroom were covered with old-fashioned newspapers, and a bare bulb over the mirror cast a harsh light. The paper towel dispenser was empty, so I wiped my mouth with the back of my hand.

"He's drunk," I said when I could talk.

"Who, Robin?" she said. She took a pin out of her piled-up hair and tucked it back in more securely, looking at herself in the mirror. "No, he's not drunk. You're the one who's drunk, Katie. Whatever possessed you to drink all that wine?"

"He said you're stupid. He said you're a mess!"

"He was kidding, Katie! You don't understand his sense of humor."

"Why are you with him? Is it because he's rich?"

She slapped me across the face. I was shocked. She had never slapped me before. "Shut up," she said in a voice I didn't know, low and full of menace. "What I do, who I date, is none of your damn business."

I held my hand against my cheek. *Then don't tell me about it*, I thought. "You remind me of Mom right now," I said. "He reminds me of Mom." She raised her hand to slap me again, but I turned away in time.

Jeannie didn't speak to me for the rest of the night. When we got to Robin's apartment, she went into a room that looked like an office, and with unnecessary force pulled a double bed out from inside a small couch. She left me there without saying goodnight. I closed the door and changed into my nightgown, then laid the clothes I planned to wear tomorrow on the back of Robin's desk chair. When I got into the bed and turned out the light, I saw that the screensaver on the computer was on. It was a picture of Robin and Jeannie at the beach, Jeannie's face turned toward Robin's and her mouth pooched into a kiss. Robin was smiling broadly with his too-white teeth. On the sand were two striped towels and a cooler full of ice and bottles; behind their heads a dark blue strip of ocean cut across an empty sky. I ached at the sight of Jeannie so happy. I felt as if I hadn't seen her in years. Maybe I was wrong about Robin. Maybe he hadn't been drunk. But because of my mother, I knew drunk when I saw it and knew the difference between joking and nasty.

Something thumped against the other side of the wall. There was a pause, then I heard it twice more. When it happened again, I put my ear against the wall but heard only my own breathing. Then it began to hit the wall every couple of seconds. My bed trembled with its repetitive force. I went to a corner on the other side of the room and sat on the rough carpet with my knees against my chest. They knew my bed was on the other side of the wall. Jeannie knew. I wondered if she'd thought about me hearing them having sex, or maybe she'd wanted me to hear.

I pressed the computer's off button until the screen went black and got back into bed. I could hear muffled voices through the wall, Jeannie's high and insistent, Robin's low, but not their words, and I was glad for that. Tomorrow, Jeannie would put me on the train back to Darien, and we wouldn't be allies anymore. Only Jeannie and I had endured our mother's rages and felt the bite of her insults. Our mother was unhappy, and I had come to believe that she wanted us to be unhappy with her. When she picked me up at the station tomorrow, she would ask why my visit was cut short. I decided to say that Jeannie had come down with a cold. I wouldn't give her the satisfaction.

I fell into a fitful doze, disturbed by the images of Robin's hand near my breasts and the angry mask of Jeannie's face. When the room grew gray with predawn light, I finally slept and had a dream in which my father appeared to me looking younger than I remembered. In a voice that seemed to enter my mind without sound, he politely asked me for permission to kill himself—"Would you allow me to die?" were his words. I was flattered he had asked me. I said he could do it. Instantly, I felt terrified. I ran into the woods shouting his name, thinking I had the power to stop him, but the woods were deeper than the woods behind our house, tangled with brambles that bloodied my legs and caught my clothes, causing me to stop and pull myself free. I saw him sitting against a tree. Who am I? I said plaintively as I approached. I wanted to hear him say my name. But he didn't say it; I was too late. My father was already dead.

VIVIAN DELMAR

For twelve years, Eleanor had been telling people her parents were dead, but the chance of that being true anytime soon was slim. Her mother had given birth to Eleanor at twenty-one; her father had been twenty-three. Now, at fifty-six and fifty-eight, respectively, they traveled around the country in a derelict RV, stopping in random towns whenever they needed money and taking what temporary work they could find. They had been living this way since Eleanor's junior year of college. Her roommate at the time referred to them, too often, as "recreational hobos." Eleanor had killed them off in a crash the summer after graduation and arrived in New York City an orphan.

Their number was identified on her cellphone by the name Vivian Delmar, which was their first names combined, and Eleanor wouldn't pick up their calls unless she was alone. "What," she'd say in an unencouraging tone. They didn't call on any particular day or time, and sometimes not for long stretches, so she always jumped a little when "Vivian Delmar" lit up the screen.

They called one evening when she was at a restaurant with a guy named Nick whom she'd been set up with by a mutual friend. The restaurant was a fashionable spot, and the crowd at the bar was deep. She looked at her phone, set it to vibrate, and dropped it back into her purse.

"It's just someone boring," she said as she dug into her pasta. It was past eight and she was ravenous. She was always eating or thinking about eating; it was a miracle she wasn't fat.

"Boring how?" Nick asked.

The question surprised her. "Oh, I don't know." She thought about an acquaintance who really was boring. "She just had a baby and can't talk about anything else. Don't you hate that?"

Nick raised an eyebrow. He had fabulous eyebrows, dark and full, and his eyes were truly aquamarine. He was handsomer than she was pretty by far, which she hoped he wouldn't realize. "Don't you like children?" he said.

"I adore children," she said. "I mean talking constantly about any subject is a bore." Mostly what she felt about children was that she needed to give birth to one soon because she would be forty in only five years. Every guy she went out with was a possible mate. She wasn't fooling around anymore. She imagined a dark-haired, aqua-eyed child, the product of Nick's dominant genes. Her hair was blond by way of the bottle, mouse-colored in its natural state. Though her eyes were identified as blue on her driver's license, they were as gray as an overcast sky.

She felt her phone vibrate where her bag touched her hip. She excused herself, went to the bathroom, and locked herself in a stall. Vivian Delmar had called three times since the day before. She sat on the toilet and listened to the voicemail.

"Eleanor sweetie?" Vivian's voice sang with eagerness. "Call us, okay? It's important." Eleanor had arrived at the opinion that Vivian was a twit when she agreed with Delmar that becoming a vagabond would be fun. She'd been a stay-at-home mom all of Eleanor's childhood, family-centric and involved in the community. "I know Dad's making you do this," Eleanor had said as plans were made and possessions sold. "Maybe I'm making him do it," Vivian had replied.

"What's the matter?" she said when Vivian answered.

"Nothing's the matter," Vivian said. "We have exciting news."

"Yeah? What?" Eleanor examined her fingernails, which had been manicured that day, and was irked by a minute bare spot in the pink polish near the cuticle of her thumb. The last "exciting news" her parents had imparted was that they had traded in their RV for a slightly less run-down model.

"We're coming to New York!" Vivian said.

"You can't do that," Eleanor said in a rigidly calm voice. "RVs aren't allowed in the city." This wasn't true, but she thought it should have been.

"The RV isn't going to be a problem. Wait, your father wants to talk to you."

"Eleanor?" She held the phone away from her ear. He had always spoken louder than was necessary. "We're going to leave the RV in New Jersey and take the bus into the city."

"Where would you stay?" Eleanor said. "Hotels are expensive, you know."

There was a silence before Delmar said, "Well, I figured we'd stay with you."

A toilet flushed and a pair of heels clacked across the tiles. Eleanor heard water running, then the rip of a paper towel. Occasionally she talked to her parents using FaceTime, but it had been a decade since she'd seen them in person. Early on, she had made an effort to visit them wherever they'd landed, staying on the narrow couch in their RV. Then one year she decided to use her vacation days to go to Cancun and had such a good time that she never visited them again.

"I'm at dinner, Dad. I can't talk about this right now."

She hung up without saying goodbye. She flushed the toilet as if she had used it and washed her hands at a row of sinks beneath a long mirror. Dampening a paper towel with cold water, she pressed it to her burning cheeks. She thought of herself as a generous host: she had a pullout couch where her out-of-town friends often stayed.

"No fucking way," she said. "Not in a million years."

The next day, she sat at her desk in the art gallery where she worked, eating an orange to keep from falling asleep and wondering how long she and Nick would have to date before she could rightfully call him her boyfriend. Like her, he was thirty-five, but that was still young for a man. He might be playing the field. Beyond the gallery's front window, pedestrians walked past in the late afternoon sun. Vivian Delmar lit up her phone for the second time that day.

"Go away," she said to the phone as she tapped "Decline." She should have turned it off but didn't want to in case Nick called. They had plans to go to an avant garde movie that night at a small theater in the Village. Dinner before or dinner after? she wondered. She could never decide which was better.

"Why are you telling your phone to go away?" said a tall, gray-haired gentleman standing in front of Eleanor's desk. She hadn't seen him walk in.

"May I help you?" She stood and smoothed the wrinkles from the lap of her skirt. She gestured toward the signage on the wall that read, *Henrik Pitzer: Reimagining Dimensions*, and said, "Have you seen our latest exhibit?"

"Yes, I bought that painting over there at the opening." He pointed to a large canvas that was smeared and splatted with various shades of yellow. "I was coming in to see it again. But now I'm much more interested in why you're talking to your phone." He smiled charmingly, a seventy-something imp. His eyes twinkled beneath the drooping flesh of his eyelids; he wore a dark jacket and tie despite the heat of the day.

"It's not that interesting. Just my parents." She shrugged.

"They won't stop calling me."

"And you won't answer?"

"It's not important," she said. "Why don't we go look at your painting?" She led him over to the wall where the canvas hung. "It's the best one, in my opinion. My favorite, really."

"I'm sure you say that to every buyer."

"I don't." She did. They stood a while in silence, looking at the painting until Eleanor's eyes throbbed. "They want to come visit me," she said.

"Your parents," he said.

She nodded.

"And you don't want them to."

"It's hard to explain why, but everybody I know thinks they're dead."

"Because that's what you've claimed?" he said.

"Yes. Is that really awful?"

"I'm going to assume they're embarrassing in some way."

"You have no idea," she said.

"Then tell me."

"They live in an RV—I mean, that's their home—and take menial jobs to get by. They used to be perfectly normal. My dad was an accountant. My mom was president of the PTA. But now they're trailer trash."

"And here you are, their elegant daughter," he said. "Living in Manhattan and working at a chic art gallery."

She stepped away. "Obviously you think I'm ridiculous for being ashamed of them, but I knew them when they wouldn't have considered living this way."

"Life is long," he said. "If I showed you a film of your future, you'd be surprised by the choices you'd see yourself making."

"What does my future have to do with my parents?"

"Very likely nothing," he said. He tipped an invisible hat to her, then walked out of the gallery and into the street, where he disappeared into the teeming rush-hour crowd.

Missy, Eleanor's boss, came over. "Who was that?"

"The guy who bought this painting," Eleanor said.

"This painting? It hasn't been sold," Missy said.

"You're kidding. Then why would he come in here and say that?"

Her phone rang. It was Vivian Delmar again. This time she blocked the number.

By Eleanor's reckoning, the theater held no more than twenty-five seats. Arriving late, she and Nick found seats in a crowded row as the credits ended and the black-and-white movie began. A tall, painfully thin man stood in a bare room with an old-fashioned cassette recorder hanging from his neck by a cord. A woman wearing a tuxedo came in and primly sat down at a piano. Just as the man pressed a button on the recorder, she began to play a quiet melody. It was hard for Eleanor to understand what was coming from the recorder. Words, but not sentences; a background clatter; the keening of some sort of animal. The film was scratched with white blips and lines. The man lifted his arms and slowly twirled to the music. The woman changed to a honky-tonk sort of tune, banging her hands hard on the keys. The man stopped twirling and, opening his mouth wide, made a whale-like sound that was even louder than the piano.

"Why on earth did you choose this movie?" Eleanor whispered irritably to Nick. It was hotter in the theater than it was outdoors. "It's so weird."

He turned in his seat and looked at her. She could barely make out his face in the dark. "I chose it because I wanted to see it. You're kind of uptight, you know that? A little weird now and then might do you some good."

Eleanor sat back as if punched. She had no idea he was so haughty. "I'm not uptight," she whispered. "Today I told a stranger the deepest secret of my life."

"Telling a stranger your deepest secret is easy," Nick said. "Try telling a friend."

"Well, aren't you the judgmental one."

The guy behind them leaned forward and said, "Pardon me for interrupting, but would you shut up?"

"You're the one who passed judgment on this film less than two minutes in." Nick turned and faced the stage. Eleanor had ceased to exist.

The thin man was talking about memory, comparing it to smoke. "Whoosh!" he said and clapped his big hands.

Eleanor closed her eyes. Sweat trickled down her spine. Abruptly, she stood up and made her way across the aisle—"Excuse me . . . pardon me . . . sorry"—and went out to the theater's dank-smelling lobby. She waited a minute to see if Nick would follow before banging out the glass doors to the street.

She walked the few blocks to the subway entrance. The doors of the train opened to a wall of passengers. She squeezed in and held on to a pole. Near Times Square the train slowed for a minute, then came to a full stop. The lights in the car dimmed; the air conditioning shuddered and sighed. The conductor's voice came over the loudspeaker and said something unintelligible.

"Sounds like he said, 'Time minds the nutty rack,'" said a woman standing next to her.

"I heard 'Don't throw the deal,'" Eleanor said. There was no indication they were going to move soon, or ever. As the heat in the car began to rise, she realized she was very hungry. She had decided on dinner after the theater because the film wasn't meant to be long. *You didn't tell me Nick is an asshole,* she imagined saying to their mutual friend. What would Nick say about her? Uptight, judgmental, a bitch.

"Do you have anything to eat?" she said to the woman.

"Excuse me?" the woman said. "You want me to give

you something to eat?"

"I'm starving," Eleanor said.

"Begging is against the law," the woman said. She flipped her long, beaded braids over her shoulder with a toss of her head. She was so tall that Eleanor had to look up at her. "Not only that, you look like you can afford your own food."

"I'm not begging," Eleanor said. "I have low blood sugar. I was just wondering if you had anything like a bag of chips."

"A bag of chips?" the woman said. "Do I look like someone who carries junk food around?"

"No, of course not," Eleanor said. "I can't believe I asked. Forgive me. It's just been, you know, a really strange day."

"Yeah, okay," the woman said. "I can relate to strange."

"I've been told I could use some weird."

The woman laughed. "Have some of mine. I got enough weird in my life for the both of us."

The lights flickered bright, and the air conditioner heaved back to life. Finally, the train moved. Through the windows, Eleanor watched the stations fly by, familiar and yet startling. She felt untethered and a little scared for herself, much as she had all those years ago when her parents drove away for what turned out to be forever. She took out her phone and unblocked their number. She half expected it to ring.

"This is my stop," she told the woman as the trained pulled into her station. "I'm sorry about before."

"Oh, wait now," the woman said. She dug into her purse, pulled out a small bag of potato chips, and handed the bag to Eleanor.

"What? No," Eleanor said. She tried to return the bag.

"Pay it forward, honey," the woman said in a jolly voice. The car doors closed, and the train growled out of the station. Eleanor looked at the bag: salt-and-vinegar flavor.

Her building was in the middle of the block midway between two streetlights. She was always nervous approaching it after dark, careful to look behind her. She stopped several yards away: there were a couple of vagrants blocking her door. *Get away from there*, she almost cried out, but stopped herself when she saw who they were.

They sat on the stoop with two suitcases at their feet. Vivian was thinner than Eleanor remembered, Delmar smaller. He looked, she thought, like a troll. Both had gone completely gray, which she'd known but hadn't thought about. They wore T-shirts, shorts, and flip-flops, like a million other people at that time of year, but the clothes looked like cast-offs they might have cadged from Goodwill, one T-shirt advertising an adventure park and the other emblazoned with the word "whatever."

"How long have you been here?" She stood before them with her arms spread, as if to block them from escaping her question. She thought of her neighbors stepping past them on their way into the building. She hoped no one had asked them who they were. But of course people had asked, or tried to shoo them away.

"Since midday," Delmar said. "We figured you'd come home eventually."

"I wish I'd known."

"If you'd known, you would have told us to get back on the next bus," Delmar said.

"I would have," Eleanor said. "Why are you here if you know I don't want you?"

"The RV is on its last legs. Basically, it's dead," Vivian said. "And we haven't seen you in nine years, Eleanor. You look so different, so . . . urbane."

Eleanor sat down between them and put her face in her hands. "Shit," she said.

"Don't cry," Vivian said. "We can go to a motel."

"That's not it," Eleanor said. She turned to her father. "I told everyone you were dead."

"Not far from it at this point," Delmar said.

"What do you mean, are you sick?"

"He's joking, sweetie," Vivian said. "He just means we're worn out."

Eleanor sighed. She felt worn out, too. She leaned into her mother and breathed deeply. Vivian smelled the same as she always had, like sugar and laundry soap. Eleanor took her father's hand, freckled now, and ropey with veins, not the hand she used to know. It made her sad that they felt worn out when they weren't even sixty yet.

She reached into her purse and found the bag of chips, offered it to her parents before eating the chips herself. A cab drove by, then a bicycle messenger. The street was unusually quiet. "There were times I needed you. Just because your kid is grown doesn't mean you can disappear."

"We didn't disappear," Vivian said. "You could always call us."

"What good is calling you when you're two thousand miles away?" Eleanor said. "I needed you in person."

"Maybe we needed you, too," Delmar said.

"Obviously you didn't," Eleanor said. "I'm not feeling sorry for you."

"We need you now," Vivian said. "But if that's not okay, we understand."

"I have to think about it," Eleanor said. She stood up and walked into the pool of light cast by the streetlamp. There were no cars coming, no pedestrians, only Vivian and Delmar and herself. She ate the last of the chips and crushed the bag in her fist. She was still hungry for something; she didn't know what.

OUTRAGEOUS

On Monday morning, in her office at the magazine, Lydia found a note on her desk. *Bitch I'm going to fuck you up the ass,* it read. The handwriting was scraggly and uncertain looking, as if whoever wrote it had used the wrong hand. The paper was the kind that was used for copies, and the ink was blue from a ballpoint pen. Because correcting errors in punctuation and grammar was what Lydia did every day, she was distracted by the lack of a comma after "bitch." She took the note to the managing editor.

"Harrison, look what I found on my desk." She affected a casual attitude because she wanted to see his surprise. His shoulders twitched as he began to read, his wisecracker face going slack.

"You found this on your desk?" he said.

"Yup." She crossed her arms over her chest. She knew what he was thinking: no man in his right mind would want to fuck a woman her age any which way, regardless of his intent. Barely qualified thirty-year-old men seemed to be running the world these days, while women like her, with decades of experience, toiled to make them look good. The magazine was about sports, and all the writers were men. Like children, they wore blue jeans, and the caps of their favorite teams, and great galumphing sneakers on their feet. Lydia wore a skirt or dressy slacks every day, and if she went out to lunch it was usually with the editor-in-chief's assistant, Ramona, a woman about her own age.

"Keep this to yourself until I find out who wrote it," Harrison said.

"Okay," Lydia said. "But how do you plan to do that?"

"Don't you worry," he said.

Lydia shrugged and tucked the note into her blazer pocket. Feathers would probably be ruffled, and she would be treated with kid gloves for a while, but nothing else would come of it, and she honestly didn't care. The threat was an empty one, of that much she was sure.

She went back to her office, turned on her computer, and began to copy edit a human-interest article about a blind discus thrower. There were so many errors that she thought about scolding the writer but decided not to when it occurred to her that her propensity for finger wagging might have been the inspiration for the note. She knew she had a reputation for being tough, but she thought she was well liked. Many times over the years, she'd been told how valuable she was. She tried to think who on the staff might have had something against her, but to her mind they were all nice enough young men, not so different from her son Lester, an executive at Facebook. Thinking about him made her feel like talking to him, so she picked up her phone and speed-dialed his number.

"Mom, it's not even seven o'clock here," he said.

"You're too busy to talk to me at work," she said. "And then you're out gallivanting at night. When else am I supposed to get a hold of you?"

"Gallivanting!" he said. "That's such a Mom word. What have you been up to?"

"This and that," she said, considering whether to tell him. Why not. "I found a filthy note on my desk this morning."

"Filthy how?"

"Nasty language, I won't repeat it. It looks like a three-year-old wrote it."

"Wait, is it threatening?"

She was pleased by the concern in his voice. She had raised him alone after she and his father divorced, and they had a close relationship: even as a teenager, he'd come to her for advice. When she'd remarried during his sophomore year of college, he'd taken against her husband. The marriage hadn't lasted long anyway. She enjoyed her independence.

"It's meant to be frightening, but I'm not in the least afraid. I'll text it to you, you can see for yourself." She took a shot of the note with her phone and sent it.

"God, Mom. This is outrageous."

"It's absurd, really. I'm fifty-eight years old."

"What does that have to do with it? Why are you laughing?"

"Someone is angry at me, that's all. It's nothing to worry about. I showed it to Harrison. You should have seen his face!"

"Listen, Mom, I have to run," Lester said.

"Okay, honey," Lydia said. He was always in such a hurry.

When she hung up the phone, she reread the note. It really was outrageous. Opening her desk drawer, she took out a pen and inserted the missing comma.

At one-thirty, Lydia's phone rang.

"Hungry?" Ramona said. "I'm dying for spicy tuna."

"Give me five minutes," Lydia said. She resealed the Tupperware container of salad she'd brought from home, put on her coat, and took the elevator down thirty floors. Ramona was waiting at the lobby security counter, flirting with the guards. She was wraith thin and bottle blond, her hair as long and wild as a hippie's; she wore four-inch heels and a low-cut top that showcased the rigid domes of her breasts. Lydia had a figure like an appliance box and had never done anything to her brownish-gray hair beyond having it shampooed and cut.

"Lyd!" Ramona hooted, as if she hadn't seen Lydia in ages. "We're going for sushi," she told the guards. Lydia ignored the guards, and they ignored her. She and Ramona walked down Sixth Avenue to Takamichi's, where a phalanx of sushi chefs worked behind a plexiglass sneeze guard.

"I went on another date with Mister Tartan," Ramona said after they were seated and served. Mister Tartan was a man she had met on eHarmony who wore a tartan tie in his profile picture. She rarely referred to her dates by their given names when discussing them with Lydia.

"I thought you'd settled on The Dentist," Lydia said. She maneuvered a slab of raw salmon onto her plate with her chopsticks. It was beautiful and disgusting at once. Sushi was good until you really thought about it.

"Didn't I tell you?" Ramona said. "The Dentist is hopeless in bed." She crammed a tuna roll into her mouth. "Missionary was the only way he would do it."

"Lord," Lydia said. "I've heard enough."

"Oh, don't be such a prude," Ramona said. "What's new with you?"

Lydia hated being asked what was new because usually nothing was. It went without saying that Ramona's life was more interesting than hers.

"Well, I do have news, but it's a secret." She took the note from a pocket inside her purse. "I found this on my desk this morning."

Ramona took the note. "No way. You did not," she said once she'd read it.

"I certainly did," Lydia said. Why was she affronted? She would have said the same thing in Ramona's place.

Ramona slid the note back across the table. "You wrote this, didn't you?"

"What? Why would I write that?" Lydia said. "For what earthly reason?"

"Because you're jealous that I have sex and you don't. You want me to think you have a stalker."

Lydia sat back. "It would never occur to me to do something like that. It doesn't even make sense. Not everything is about you, by the way."

"What do you mean by that?" Ramona said. "We talk about your life all the time. There's nothing I haven't heard about Lester; you go on about him nonstop."

Lydia paused a moment before saying, "At least I have a child to talk about."

Ramona stared. "I can't believe you said that."

"I can't believe you think I'd write something like this."

"Why is it a secret?" Ramona said.

"It's a secret because I brought it to Harrison as soon as I found it, and he told me not to talk to anyone about it until he finds out who wrote it."

"You took it to Harrison?"

"Of course I did," Lydia said. "I thought he should know that someone in the office is writing lewd notes."

"Harrison was humoring you, Lydia, don't be an idiot."

"He wasn't," Lydia said.

"The guys make fun of you, you know," Ramona said. She blinked her eyes rapidly several times, the way Lydia did when she was nervous. "They imitate your tic behind your back. I've told them to knock it off, but they think it's funny."

Helplessly, Lydia blinked. She'd had the tic for as long as she could remember. "I don't believe you. You're making that up."

"No, you're making that up," Ramona said, pointing at the note.

Lydia focused on Ramona's glistening lips, clownishly plumped by some sort of filler and painted a dusky maroon. She must have been gossiped about amongst the staff, a woman pushing sixty trying to look thirty years younger, but Lydia had never heard anything derogatory about her. She cast around for an insult.

"Everyone says you look like a trollop."

Ramona laughed loudly. "Oh Lydia, how ridiculous. A trollop! No one would use that word except you." She rummaged in her bag and took out her wallet. "This is for my half," she said, dropping a twenty-dollar bill on the table. She stood and walked away.

Lydia calmly continued eating. People wouldn't think anything about Ramona leaving; she might have had an appointment she had to rush off to or was late for a meeting at work. Lydia and Ramona had never had a falling-out before. They worked in the same office, but not with each other, so there was nothing to fall out about. Lydia looked around at the other customers and saw four writers from the magazine sitting at a nearby table. She caught their attention and smiled. They smiled back at her, waving hello. Any one of them could have written the note.

When she left Takamichi's, Lydia stood on the sidewalk debating whether to go to a nearby deli and buy a pack of cigarettes. Though she wasn't really a smoker anymore, she still had the occasional craving. Likewise with alcohol: she rarely drank it. But she wanted to smoke a cigarette and drink a Manhattan right now, and she didn't see why she shouldn't. She bought a pack of Marlboros and walked down 49th Street to a bar, visible through a plate glass window, that she passed every day on her way to the office. The bar was new and swanky, with low gilded tables and velvet sofas. But sitting on a sofa alone would make her look as if she were waiting for someone to join her; when no one showed up, it would seem like she'd been jilted. She sat on a very comfortable stool at the bar, ordered a drink, and lit up.

"No smoking in here," the bartender said.

Lydia looked behind her. There was no one else in the

place but two men at the far end of the room. She could barely make them out. Silvery, semi-sheer curtains had been drawn over the window, creating a twilight atmosphere. "Oh, please let me, I'm desperate," she said. "Just one?"

"Okay, one," he said.

She took a sip of her drink. There simply wasn't a better combination of chemicals than alcohol and nicotine, sedation and stimulation deliciously entwined. She wondered if she and Ramona would make up. What else could they do? She decided to apologize first, even though she had nothing to be sorry about. Ramona had thrown the first punch by accusing her of sexual envy. Hardly! Lydia didn't even like sex; the idea of being with a man made her cringe. When she was younger, yes, she'd loved it. She'd had a healthy libido. In fact, she'd been quite promiscuous until she'd gotten pregnant with Lester—before she'd married his father, even— but she wasn't going to brag to Ramona about it. Bragging was Ramona's domain.

"Do you mind if I bum one?" someone said. Lydia swiveled around. A young woman sat on the adjacent stool. She wore black leather pants and a silky gold turtleneck; her face was heavily made up. She truly looked the way Ramona wanted to look: long blond hair, lithe body, thick-lashed feline eyes. She smiled at Lydia and said in a husky voice, "Bum a cigarette, I mean."

"We're not supposed to smoke," Lydia said.

"And yet we are smoking," the woman said as she took a cigarette and lit it. "I've never seen you here before."

"No," Lydia said. "Are you here often?"

"Fairly often." She took a drag and let the smoke drift out of her mouth.

"It's a nice place," Lydia said for want of anything better to say. "I don't normally drink in the middle of the day. I don't drink at all, really. But it's been a bad day, and I feel fed up."

"About what?" the woman said. "If you don't mind my asking."

"Oh, something happened at work, then my friend and I had an argument about it."

The bartender appeared. "Hey, Dade."

"Hey, Bruce," the woman said. She turned back to Lydia. "So what's this thing that happened at work?"

Lydia ground out her cigarette in a saucer the bartender had provided. "Someone left an obscene note on my desk."

"What do you mean, obscene?"

"I can show it to you."

"Oh my," the woman said as she read the note. "Up the ass, no less!"

"I showed it to my boss, but my friend says he didn't take me seriously. She thought I wrote it myself!"

"How stupid," the woman said. "People are such shit."

The under-lit bottles behind the bar blurred into a glowing, multi-hued wall. Lydia didn't want to embarrass herself by crying, but tears welled in her eyes. Why had she been the recipient of the note? It was monstrously unfair. She'd never hurt anyone in her life. She gripped the beveled edge of the bar as if it were the railing of a ship at sea.

The woman tapped the note with a glittery red fingernail. "This is sexual harassment, you know."

"Oh no, not really," Lydia said.

"Yes, really."

Lydia considered this for a minute. "I didn't take it as seriously as that, but I guess you're right. What should I do about it?"

"Demand action," the woman said. She crossed her legs and blew out a stream of smoke. "Whoever wrote it should be fired. You have a right to a safe workplace."

"I doubt they can find out who it was."

"Then call your lawyer," the woman said. "You can sue the company, make enough money to retire." She raised her chin and closed her eyes. "If it were me, I'd move to Paris and live on the Left Bank and wear a different Hermès scarf every day."

"I always wanted to try my hand at writing a mystery novel," Lydia said. "You know, like Agatha Christie or Ruth Rendell. I think I'd be pretty good at it."

"There you go!" the woman said. "You could do anything you damn well please."

What a generous woman, Lydia thought. She couldn't remember feeling so encouraged.

"I didn't introduce myself. I'm Lydia."

"I'm Dade."

"What an unusual name," Lydia said.

"It's short for David."

"I've never heard of a woman named David."

Dade raised her eyebrows. "Oh, come on. Can you seriously not tell?"

"Tell what?" Lydia said.

"That I'm a man?" Dade said.

"A man!" Lydia said. Now she could see islands of shadow on Dade's cheeks where her beard was covered by a thick layer of foundation. The revelation made her feel momentarily confused. "So that's why you're wearing so much makeup."

Gingerly, Dade touched her face. "Do you think it's too much?"

"What do I know about makeup," Lydia said. "Gosh, your hair is amazing."

"It's a wig," Dade said. Lydia reached out and touched it. "It feels real."

"Oh, it's real hair, just not my hair," Dade said. "It cost a fortune."

"I never would have guessed you're a man if you hadn't told me," Lydia said.

"I can't tell you what a compliment that is," Dade said.

"But you would have realized eventually. It's pretty dark in here, and you're obviously too nice to think anyone is pretending to be something they're not."

"I'm not that nice," Lydia said.

The bartender came over. "Another round, ladies?"

"You bet," Dade said. "Live large! Don't you think so, Lydia?"

"Absolutely," Lydia said. She looked at her phone: half past three. She hadn't received any texts or calls. She could have been mugged and murdered for all anyone at the magazine cared. She took a mental inventory of the work on her desk and decided it could wait.

By the time Lydia returned to work, nearly everyone had gone home. Offices were dark, computer screens blank; Ramona's desk outside the editor-in-chief's door was battened down for the night. Harrison was putting on his coat when Lydia walked in.

"Lydia, you're still here?" he said. "What time is it, anyway?"

"I have no idea," Lydia said. She glanced out the window at the building across the street where a middle-aged woman sat behind a computer. Just like me, Lydia thought. Except she wasn't middle-aged anymore; she would be sixty in a couple of years. "Have you found the person who wrote the note?"

"Note?" Harrison said. He picked up a leather briefcase and placed it on his desk. The desk was covered with the proofs of the magazine's next issue that Lydia had gone over with a fine-toothed comb.

"The note I showed you this morning."

"Oh, right."

"You didn't even try," she said. "You have no such intention."

"Well, Lydia, let's be realistic. Anyone with access to your office could have written that note."

Lydia took the folded note from her purse and held it before her like a flag. "This is sexual harassment."

"Lydia, come on. There's a big difference between an anonymous note and sexual harassment."

"What if your wife received a note like this? How do you think she'd feel?"

"My wife doesn't—" He stopped and sniffed. "Have you been drinking?"

"I have," she said. "What of it?"

"Okay, let's have this conversation tomorrow. I think you'll see things differently then."

"It's outrageous!" Lydia said.

Harrison nodded. "Absolutely it is. No question."

He was humoring her. Ramona was right. She turned away. The woman in the next building crumpled a piece of paper and tossed it expertly into a wastebasket several feet from her desk, as if she'd put the wastebasket there as a challenge to herself.

"I've worked here for fourteen years. I thought I was a valued member of the staff. I'm going to have to call my lawyer about this. I have a right to feel safe at work." She turned back to Harrison. He had left the room. She went out into the hallway. He was gone.

She took the elevator to the lobby and returned to the bar. It was crowded now with beautiful young people, mostly men. The seat she'd had earlier was occupied. She found another seat at the far corner. It was very loud.

"I didn't expect to see you again," the bartender shouted.

"Where is Dade?"

"She left a few minutes ago."

"Maybe I'll have a drink before I go home," Lydia said. Permanent inebriation seemed like a good idea now that she'd gotten started.

The bartender put his elbows on the bar and folded his hands beneath his chin. He was handsome in a cherubic way, one golden curl hanging over his forehead.

"It's Lydia, right?" he said. Lydia nodded. "Lydia, this is a gay bar, but you're welcome to hang out if you want."

"Oh, I didn't realize," Lydia said.

The bartender grinned. "You learn something new every day, huh?"

"Today especially," she said.

She gave her seat to someone else and made her way through the crowd. Outside, the air smelled like snow, though it wouldn't snow, or not very much, nothing like the deep, pristine blankets of her childhood. She walked to the subway and waited on the edge of the platform for a downtown train. There were only a few other people in the station. No one was looking at her. Leaning over the tracks to see if a train was approaching, she saw headlights far down the tunnel. She watched as they grew larger and brighter, until the train was nearly at the station. She opened her purse and took out the note. Just as the train pulled abreast of the platform, she flung it out over the tracks. Flashing white in the headlights, it flew on a gust, starkly illuminated before vanishing at last.

JUNE

At ninety-one, June Hallet was still fit enough to take a taxi by herself to the hairdresser, Bloomingdale's, or a concert at Carnegie Hall, anywhere she had a mind to go. New York was an easy place to be old. There was no need to drive, and groceries could be delivered. The doormen at her building were helpful. Most of her friends and acquaintances were long gone, but a few were still hanging on: Betsy Friary and Loretta Pimm and their husbands, whom she'd known since their children were in school, and her downstairs neighbor and boon companion, Nancy Ulster, who was only two years younger. Being elderly was a constant surprise, something June forgot about until her joints throbbed or she saw her face in a mirror, deeply crosshatched and sagging like an old hound's, or when her sixty-two-year-old daughter Jessie shouted at her. "Good morning, Mother!" Jessie would hoot into the phone from Kansas City. "How are you feeling today?" enunciating each word as if English were June's second language. More or less, she felt the same today as she felt yesterday and the day before, but one of these mornings she would feel weak or ill, or take a fall, and it would all be downhill from there.

The apartment next door to June's place had been empty for four months. One afternoon in August, as June was unlocking her door, a young woman came out into the hall with a green carryall bag in her hand.

"Hello," she said. "I'm Rebecca."

"Do you live in that apartment?" June said. Rebecca might have been a realtor. Realtors had been coming in and out with prospective buyers all summer.

"My husband and I moved in yesterday," Rebecca said.

"Do you have children?" June said warily.

"No," Rebecca said. "We just got married."

"Then it's a pleasure to meet you," June said and extended her hand. The girl had a surprisingly firm grip, squeezing June's old bones. The middle-aged couple who used to live next door had been kind to June, bringing up the mail from downstairs so June wouldn't have to make the trip. She doubted Rebecca would be as nice as the Worthingtons—young people were rarely considerate—but just as the thought came to her mind, Rebecca showed June her carryall.

"I'm going to the store; can I get you anything?"

"I do need a quart of milk," June said. "I just ran out this morning. If it's not too much trouble."

"Back in a flash," Rebecca said and walked off to the elevator, swinging her bag.

June waited a minute and took the elevator herself. She got out on the ground floor and went outside, where a hot breeze from the river threw a speck of soot into her eye. Sanjay was standing beneath the awning, looking like an admiral in his dark blue uniform and cap.

"Who are the people that just moved in next door to me?" June said, blinking away the speck.

"You mean the Rosenbergs?" Sanjay said.

"Jews," June said. "You know, there was a time when Jews weren't allowed to live in this building. It's just a fact, I'm not saying it was right."

"There was a time when only whites could be doormen," Sanjay said.

June patted his arm. "That wasn't right either."

She went back inside and took the elevator to the third floor, where Nancy Ulster lived. Nancy never locked her door, so June let herself in. The apartment was laid out like June's on the floor just above, a one-bedroom with an eat-in kitchen, a dining room, and a living room. It was decorated in much the same way as June's, with antique side tables and upholstered chairs, and pretty china lamps that would cost a fortune now. Nancy was an art enthusiast who had a lot of paintings on her walls. Her hobby was stitching needlepoint pillows with flowers and animals and amusing phrases.

"I've got a new neighbor," June said as Nancy came out of the kitchen. Nancy handed June a steaming cup of tea and went back into the kitchen to make herself another. Though she and June were roughly the same height, Nancy was stouter. She tended to hunch, as she was doing now while pouring water from the kettle.

"I saw the moving van out front yesterday," she said. "Young people, yes? That's what Sanjay told me."

"Sanjay, what a treasure," June said.

"Lovely man," Nancy said. They settled into two chairs on either side of a low coffee table and sipped their tea in comfortable silence.

"The new couple's name is Rosenberg," June said after a while.

"It's about time there was some young blood in this building," Nancy said. "I don't care what their religion is."

"I couldn't agree more," June said. Rebecca might be back with the milk by now. She would go by later to pick it up and see what sort of furniture they had.

"You know, I have the strangest fluttering feeling in my neck," Nancy said. She put her teacup on the coffee table and pressed her hand to the spot. "Right here."

"Have you been good about taking your thyroid pills?" June said. Nancy sometimes forgot. June never forgot to take her pills, but then how would she know if she had?

Her daughter had been pestering her about hiring an aide to come in and help with this and that. "This and that" had been Jessie's words exactly. June thought she'd go crazy with some stranger sitting in her living room waiting for her to need something.

"I bought a pillbox that has compartments for the days of the week," Nancy said. "It's idiot proof." All of a sudden, her head tilted sideways and she melted into her chair.

"Dear, are you all right?" June said. When Nancy didn't answer, June got up and went to her. She shook Nancy by the shoulder and said her name. "Hang on, Nance, not to worry." She picked up the receiver of Nancy's ancient beige touch-tone and called the number for the lobby.

"22 East 68th Street," Sanjay said.

"Sanjay, it's Mrs. Hallet. I'm at Mrs. Ulster's and she's having some trouble. Please come up here immediately." She hung up and went back to her seat. "Sanjay is on his way," she said. "Everything is under control." She sat very straight with her hands clasped in her lap, gazing at the pattern on Nancy's faded Persian carpet. She was afraid she might cry if she looked at Nancy, which was stupid because Sanjay would be here any second.

Sanjay came in and went straight to Nancy whose eyes were glassy and face had turned gray.

"Oh, Mrs. Ulster," he said. He looked at June. "You okay, Mrs. Hallet?"

"Don't worry about me," June said almost angrily. "It's Mrs. Ulster who needs help."

"*Om shanti*, Mrs. Ulster," Sanjay said and closed Nancy's eyes with his hand.

It fell to June to inform Nancy's two sons, who lived in New Orleans and Houston, respectively.

"You must let me know if I can do anything," she

said to the Houston son. "Nancy worshiped at St. Thomas Episcopal. I suppose you'll have the service there."

"We'll have a memorial at some point," the son said.

"Some point?" June said.

"Something small down here, just the family. She didn't have any friends left to speak of."

"She was my friend," June said. "Feel free to speak of me. We saw each other every day."

He responded automatically. "I'm sorry for your loss."

So she was left to mourn Nancy alone and without ceremony. Betsy and Loretta had hardly known her, and Jessie not at all. Sanjay was sympathetic, but Nancy hadn't been the first elderly tenant to pass away on his watch: dying was what old people did. June sat in her apartment and cried for a week, then pulled herself together and began going to the park on fine afternoons and making conversation with whomever joined her on her favorite bench near the zoo. Sometimes it would be another elderly person, or a vagrant burdened by bags; usually it was an exhausted mother pushing a stroller. June considered getting a little dog, a mature rescue, but only big dogs were available at the local shelter. Then she decided a dog was too much trouble. She would have to ask Sanjay to walk it after dark, and she didn't want to be doddering and needy.

The distraction of television made evenings less lonely. She and Nancy had been loyal fans of *Masterpiece Theater* and had watched old movies together, but there were so many other good programs these days. She remembered when there were only three stations and wondered how anyone had survived. At ten o'clock, she would turn it off and call Jessie. They'd gotten into the habit of a nightly chat; Nancy's death had brought them closer.

"I don't think that fat man on *The Voice* is at all talented," she said one night in September. "I think he's a show-off, all that jiggling around."

"Ugh, he's terrible," Jessie said. "I'm rooting for the girl with the guitar."

Something banged hard against the wall from the apartment next door, causing June to jump. "How odd," she said to Jessie. She'd never heard a peep out of the Rosenbergs before.

After a few more minutes, they said goodbye and June got ready for bed. When she went into the kitchen to pour herself some water, she heard another noise from next door. Muffled voices, a crash, the sound of something shattering. Though she continued to listen, there was no other sound but the trickling of water passing through the pipes in the wall.

The next day as she was going out to have a cup of coffee at a bakery around the corner, she saw Rebecca in the mail room, sorting through letters. As June approached, Rebecca turned away as if avoiding her. But it was too late for June to retreat.

"We haven't talked since you brought me the milk that day!" she said. She had been surprised to find the carton at her door after poor Nancy's body had been taken away.

"Life, right?" Rebecca said vaguely. She continued sorting through mail as if June wasn't standing right there.

"I didn't think young people had anything to do with mail anymore," June said, determined to have a conversation. The room was bright, lit by a block of fluorescent tubes. The mail slots were built into one wall; a bench on the other side of the room was piled with packages. "I thought it was all texting and twitting these days."

Rebecca smiled and looked up. "You mean tweeting," she said. There was a blue bruise just beneath the socket of her right eye.

"My goodness, what happened to you?" June said.

"What do you mean?"

June looked pointedly at the bruise.

"Oh, this." Rebecca touched the bruise with exploratory fingers. Her long nails were painted dark red. She was really quite pretty. A little too done up, but nice looking beneath all that eye shadow and blush. "I smacked my face with my blow dryer," she said. "Can you believe how stupid that is?"

I don't believe it at all, June thought. "I heard a lot of noise from your apartment last night."

"What do you mean?" Rebecca said.

"Some knocking about, a crash."

"Oh, we were unpacking our china, I dropped a plate. I hope we didn't bother—"

"Oh, no," June said. "You didn't bother me at all."

Rebecca made a show of looking at her watch and claimed she was running late. Wristwatches were another thing June had thought young people eschewed. Mail and watches and photographs you could frame. But some things didn't change; human nature was always the same. June walked out into the cool, overcast day and stood on the pavement beside Sanjay.

"What do you know about Mr. Rosenberg?" she said.

"Mr. Rosenberg? Nice man, very friendly. Why do you ask?"

"I think he's beating up his wife."

Sanjay looked at her in surprise. "Oh, now, Mrs. Hallet. The Rosenbergs are newlyweds! Have you seen them together? They're in love!"

"I've only seen her, not him. I heard a ruckus in their apartment last night and she's got a bruise on her face today."

Sanjay whistled softly through his teeth and looked down the street. There was a gaggle of private school boys on their way home from school, their uniform neckties loose and their shirttails hanging out. "How've you been holding up since Mrs. Ulster passed?" he said.

"Don't change the subject," she said. "Something ought to be done."

"Mrs. Hallet, no offense," Sanjay said. "But I'm sure you're mistaken."

"I doubt it," June said. She didn't feel like a coffee anymore, but she walked on to the bakery anyway. The bakery, then the library, where she'd browse the stacks for an hour. Then she'd have to come up with some other way to occupy herself.

The Rosenbergs were quiet for a long while after that, and June decided Sanjay was right. But on Halloween she heard voices again through the wall, one deep and one faint. They were probably having a party, she told herself at first, or they had the television on very loud. The deep voice was constant. The faint one could barely be heard. There was a sudden shout and a thumping sound that made June jump back as if stung. She went out into the hall and stood there undecided. She could ring their bell, but then what? Or she could go back to her apartment and watch her show. She rang the bell. Immediately, Mr. Rosenberg answered the door, wearing a business suit but not a tie. He was a tall man—in his late twenties, June judged. He held a bowl of miniature candy bars for the trick or treaters in the building, though the trick or treaters had been and gone long before dinnertime.

"Hello," he said in a matter-of-fact voice, as if they met every day.

"I'm Mrs. Hallet from next door."

"Nice to meet you," he said, showing a row of perfect teeth. "How may I help you?"

"Oh," she said. He seemed so normal. The television was in fact on. "I thought, well, I should introduce myself. I've met your lovely wife already."

"Terrific. I'll tell her you were here. Thank you for coming by." Without further comment, he closed the door.

"How astonishing," June said. She went back to her

apartment, picked up the phone, and called Jessie.

"Is everything all right?" Jessie said, because it wasn't their usual time.

"Yes and no," June said. "I'm fine, but my neighbor is beating up his wife."

"What?" Jessie said. "How on earth do you know that?"

"I can hear them, for one thing," June said. "A few weeks ago, there was a lot of banging around in their apartment and then I saw the woman the next day. She had a bruise on her face. She didn't want to speak to me, she turned away, said she'd hit her face with her hair dryer. Then tonight, just a few minutes ago, I heard them arguing again. There was a scream and then it sounded like something hit the floor."

Jessie was silent. "Mother," she said and was silent again.

"You don't believe me," June said.

"Neighbors make all sorts of noises. Maybe they were roughhousing, fooling around. You told me they're young. Who knows what they were up to."

"I know what a man hitting a woman sounds like," June said. She was surprised to hear her voice tremble. "I know when a bruise is more than just a bruise."

"Oh, come on, Mom. How would you know that?"

June closed her eyes. "I wouldn't, really."

"You miss Nancy," Jessie said.

"Of course I do," June said briskly. "Listen, my TV show is about to start. I'll call you when it's over."

She turned on the television and watched without listening. She had thought her first husband was the love of her life until he hit her two months after they married for the sin of correcting his grammar. He'd caught her on her cheekbone with his knuckles and given her a nasty welt that looked much like the bruise on Rebecca's face. Like Rebecca, she'd lied about how she got it. Her parents hadn't liked him for no reason they could name, and she couldn't bring herself to admit they'd been right. And she'd loved him! She had. And believed he loved her. She'd been all of twenty-two.

He didn't hit her again for nearly a year—she'd gotten over it, moved on—then he started hitting her all the time. Eighteen months later, he broke two of her ribs. She left him then, and moved to the city, got a job, and started over. He gave her a split lip for suggesting they divorce, but he hadn't gone after her when she finally defected, as brutal men often did. Jessie didn't know about June's first husband. Nancy had known, of course. Nancy knew everything about June, and June knew everything about Nancy.

Her reverie was broken by another loud argument next door. She picked up the phone and called Sanjay.

"The Rosenbergs are making a racket," she told him. "I wish you'd come up here and listen to this."

"I'll give them a call, Mrs. Hallet," Sanjay said.

"No, I want you to hear them," June said. "Just so you don't think I'm crazy."

"I don't think you're crazy, Mrs. Hallet."

"He's hitting her, Sanjay, I know it."

"No, I don't think so," Sanjay said. "I'll be up in a minute."

Whatever did happen to her first husband? she wondered. Had he remarried and abused another woman? Perhaps it had been only she who'd driven him to violence. She was grateful there hadn't been children to tie them for life. He was dead now, most likely. She hoped he was in Hell.

By the time Sanjay knocked on her door, the Rosenbergs were quiet.

"Now you do think I'm crazy," June said. "But they were at it not two minutes ago."

Sanjoy took off his cap. June was surprised he was going bald; she'd never seen him bareheaded before. "Mrs. Hallet, couples argue," he said.

"I know that!" June said. "Couples argue, but they usually don't fall on the floor while they're doing it. They don't break things. These walls are paper thin, I can hear everything."

"I'll have a word with them," Sanjay said. "I'll ask them to keep it down."

When he left, she went to the door and put her ear against it. She didn't hear anything. He might well have just gone back downstairs.

Jessie called at ten o'clock.

"I have something to tell you," June said before her daughter could speak. "I was married before I met your father."

"Excuse me?" Jessie said. "What?"

"You heard me," June said.

"Mother, I think it's really time we discussed your situation," Jessie said. "I think you should move out here. There's a terrific assisted-living complex down the street from us."

"I was married to a man who physically abused me," June said. "It was terrible, but I left him eventually. I met your father a few years later."

"What was his name?" Jessie said.

June moved to the edge of her chair and turned off the TV. "What difference does that make? Why do you want to know?"

"Just tell me."

"All right. His name was Garrett Price."

"If this is true—"

"Of course it's true," June said. She could hear Jessie sigh. "Why would I lie?"

"I'm not saying you're lying, Mother. But why is this the first I'm hearing of it? Why didn't you or Dad tell me before?"

"Your father didn't know," June said. She got up and went to a shelf where she displayed her framed photographs. There was one of Jessie's late father standing with Jessie at her wedding, both of them looking delighted and very much like each other: they would have been identical if Jessie had been a boy. June's second husband wouldn't have comprehended a man like Garrett Price. "He was such a wonderful person, your father. I didn't deserve him, or that was how I felt. I was desperately ashamed of myself."

"Mom, don't get upset," Jessie said.

"I'm not upset," June said. "I'm speaking the truth. I'm ninety-one years old, for God's sake."

"Exactly," Jessie said. "If you don't want to move out here, then I think it's time we got you that aide we talked about."

"I didn't talk about it, you did," June said. She touched the frame of a cracked and faded black-and-white photograph: herself as a teenager, smiling into the sun. "I'm talking about something else right now. I'm talking about my life."

Her head ached when she woke the next day; her eyes felt sandy and swollen. She lay in bed reading and then letting her mind wander, listening to the radio on her nightstand. Fitfully, she dozed, dreaming of people she'd never known, dogs in cages like the ones at the shelter, a merry-go-round she'd loved as a child. Around eleven o'clock, she was startled awake by the insistent buzz of the doorbell. She answered in her bathrobe.

Rebecca Rosenberg was standing in the hallway holding the same green carryall she'd had when June first met her, this time filled with groceries. Her face was ugly with anger.

"Sanjay told me what you've been saying," she said. "How dare you. You don't know the first thing about us."

"I know what I hear," June said. "I know what I see." She put her hands in the pockets of her robe. A draft was coming in from the hall. There were yellow marks on Rebecca's neck, ghosts of old bruises. "My husband used to strangle me, too. It's terrible, isn't it, that feeling of not being able to breathe, wondering if this time he'll actually kill you. But he won't kill you, because who would he have to knock around if you were dead?"

"You're hallucinating," Rebecca said. "Sanjay says you're going senile."

"That's an easy thing to say about someone my age," June said. "I was your age, a bit younger, when my husband began to hit me. Not long after the wedding. He was charming before we got married. I suppose your husband was too, or you wouldn't have married him. But I got away. I found someone else, had a daughter. You can get away too. You're young enough to start again."

"Mind your own business," Rebecca said.

"You are my business," June said. "Women like us have to help each other. You're not alone. I'll be here when you need me."

"I don't need you," Rebecca said. She hoisted the carryall over her shoulder. "You're deluding yourself, old lady." She turned and went into her own apartment.

June stared for a moment at the deserted hall before closing the door. Returning to her bedroom, she lay down in the warm indentation she'd made in the bed. She would have to tell Nancy about the Rosenbergs, she thought before remembering Nancy was dead. She touched her forehead with the back of her hand. She felt weak, not quite well.

DANCE, ROCKETTE

The cottage was only a rental for the month of August, so it wasn't up to Eve to keep the garden alive, but it had been hotter than usual for a couple of days and the blue hydrangeas that flanked the front door were drooping tragically in the late afternoon sun. She got the hose and sprayed them down, then went around back and watered the roses. The children were out on the lawn playing a game with their babysitter, Mattie, who was the seventeen-year-old daughter of friends in the city. If she'd had her druthers, they'd have gone someplace livelier than Connecticut, but her husband, Rick, had fond memories of growing up in Old Lyme, and it was an easy commute from the city. For the past three weeks he'd been spending long weekends out here, arriving by train late on Thursdays and going back to Manhattan Monday mornings, but starting today he would be staying all week. It was the last week, the end of summer.

She went inside and upstairs to her bedroom, where she put on a peach-and-white-flowered blouse and a pair of slim white pants. Orange sandals and her strand of south sea pearls, gold earrings in the shape of scallop shells; as she brushed her dark hair, she noticed a rime of gray roots that would necessitate a trip to the salon as soon as she got back to the city. She assessed her appearance in the mirror. Chic or dumpy? A little of both. Almost immediately after her fiftieth birthday, or so it seemed, her bright-eyed prettiness had faded, but she couldn't complain; she'd had her day.

She drove over the bridge that spanned the Connecticut River, wide here where it met Long Island Sound, the marshlands emerald, the water slate gray, the cloudless horizon glowing pink. She turned into the train station lot and parked facing the platform so Rick would see her when he disembarked. Rummaging in her purse, she got out of the car and lit a cigarette. The kids would go crazy if they knew she occasionally smoked, but Rick didn't care. She inhaled deeply. She had five minutes to herself. Rick might have bought a few beers at Grand Central to drink on the trip, in which case he'd be blurry when he got off the train. But he'd been looking forward to this evening at the Rosses' all week—Ben Ross was his old high school pal—so perhaps he'd remained sober this evening in anticipation of a better drink.

The train was announced and after a few minutes arrived. Rick was the second passenger out. Eve waved and watched him come down the ramp. He'd loosened his tie but looked otherwise tidy.

"Right on time," she said as she ground out her cigarette with her heel.

"I thought we were going straight to the party," he said.

"We are," she said.

"But you need to change," he said.

She looked down at herself. "This is what I'm wearing."

"Do you think it's dressy enough?"

"What did you expect, a tiara?" She knew what he was thinking. Ben Ross had invented some small but necessary technological widget that had made him wealthy, and while she and Rick were well-off enough to live in a three-bedroom on the Upper East Side, Rick had struggled along the way, moving firms twice before finally making partner. Renting the cottage for a whole month had been a bit of a stretch. Eve guessed Ben's good fortune had gotten under

Rick's skin. He and Ben had been playing tennis at Ben's club every Saturday morning, riding there together in Ben's sleek black Ferrari. "I think I look nice," she said. "I'm wearing the earrings you gave me."

"I didn't say you don't look nice," he said as he got into the driver's seat. Eve handed him the keys. "But I think Ben and his wife might be expecting us to be dressier."

"It's better to be underdressed than overdressed," Eve said.

He started the car and drove out of the lot. "I think it's better to be just right."

"Okay, Goldilocks. Do you want to go home so I can change?"

"We're already late," he said.

"Better to be late than early."

"What's with you tonight?"

"Nothing. What's with you?" He didn't answer. She looked out at the river. Mattie was bored, the kids were bored, she was bored. The pleasures of Old Lyme had long been exhausted. They were all looking forward to going home. She wondered if Rick had found whatever he'd been looking for by returning to the halcyon scene of his youth. But Rick was a simple guy, meat and potatoes, not given to self-reflection.

The Rosses' house was reached by a narrow road that wound through a forest of oaks. Nothing had been done in the way of landscaping, and the road was unpaved and bumpy. A branch scraped the side of the car; rocks flew up from beneath the tires. A deer flitted past. There was a sudden odor of skunk. Finally, the road widened, and a stone cottage appeared.

"How sweet," Eve said. It had a charming, rose-covered trellis.

"That's not their house," Rick said. "That's the caretaker's cottage." *Of course it is,* Eve thought. Rick drove on for a few more minutes until they reached a white-pebbled drive that led to a three-story, gray-shingled house. Four cars were parked on the edge of the drive. Rick pulled up behind the last one. "That's the house," he said unnecessarily.

"Well, that is some house," Eve said. She'd never seen a house with a widow's walk before. But the house wasn't old, the widow's walk was an affectation: no one had ever used it to scout for homecoming vessels. A flight of steps took them up to a deep porch that was furnished with a row of wicker rockers like the veranda of a seaside hotel.

Rick knocked on the side of the screen door. "Hello!" he called into an empty front hall.

"Hang on!" came a woman's voice, and then the woman herself. She wore what appeared to be a knee-length, very tight, pink-and-white-striped T-shirt, her pelvic bones popping out like knobs, and a pair of pink high-heeled sandals that looked impossible to walk in. Her hair was long and thick and reddish blond, cascading down her back. Diamond earrings in the shape of chandeliers swung fetchingly from her ears. "Well, don't just stand there, come in!" she said. "I'm Helene, Ben's wife."

His first wife? Eve wondered. Surely not, she was too young. "We're Eve and Rick," she said.

"Oh, I know," said Helene. "Come on, follow me. We're all out back."

They went through a large living room that was furnished almost entirely in white—*no pets or children,* was Eve's first thought—and out onto a flagstone terrace. A glass-topped table was set for eight, with a tiny vase containing a pink rose at each place. Candles in crystal cylinders stood in a line down the center of the table. The silverware appeared to really be silver, sparking in the last light.

"What a beautiful view of the river!" Eve said.

"We're on a bluff," Helene said. She pointed to where a flight of wooden steps began. "Those steps over there go down to our dock."

"You have a boat," Rick said as if he already knew it.

"Yes, but we hardly ever use it. There are so many other things to do."

Such as? Eve wondered. She would enjoy a boat ride. Maybe Ben would take her on one if she asked him. He stood on the lawn with a woman and three men who all had drinks in their hands.

"Buddy!" he called and came over to Rick.

"I don't want to rush anyone," Helene said. "But Gladys says dinner is ready." Now Eve could see she wasn't so young after all. Forty-five at least. Obviously, she'd had work done on her face: her skin stretched taut over her cheekbones and sharp little nose, her forehead was smooth, her lips artificially plump. Her breasts were the size and shape of cantaloupes, revealed by the deep scoop of her neckline. Ben was a big guy with a considerable belly. Helene was painfully thin. She waved her arm as if to corral her guests. "Everyone, come on!"

The man and the woman were husband and wife, and the two men lived together. Tad and Gina and Timothy and Pete. Tad and Gina were Helene's "oldest friends in the whole wide world." Timothy and Pete were merely neighbors.

"Ben and Rick went to Old Lyme High together," Helene said. She sat at the head of the table, Ben at the other end. Eve was sandwiched between Timothy and Tad. The table was meant to hold six, but they were eight. Eve would have thought she and Rick were the odd ones out if they hadn't been invited last week.

"Rick was cool," Ben said. "I was a loser."

"Now Ben is cool," Rick said.

"And you're the loser?" Pete said.

"I'm an attorney," Rick said. He picked up the empty

wine glass by his plate and looked at it with disappointment.

"No, I mean, obviously I'm joking," Pete said.

Timothy turned to Eve. "You live in Manhattan? And what do you do?"

"I take care of our children," Eve said. "A boy and a girl."

"I would have thought your children would be grown up," Gina said. "Ours are, more or less." Like Eve, she wore linen slacks and a casual blouse. *So there,* Eve thought, *I'm not underdressed.*

"I came late to motherhood," she said. "I was thirty-eight when I had my first."

Pete looked at her over the top of his eyeglasses. "You must have done something before coming late to mother-hood."

Eve paused. *I really can't stand you,* she thought. "I was a Rockette," she said. Rick stared at her.

"No way!" Gina said. "Wow!"

"You never told me that," Ben said to Rick.

"It's ancient history," Eve said. "I don't talk about it much. It's hard on your body as you can imagine. I had to stay in tip-top shape all the time. And the constant rehearsals and spectaculars—well, let's just say the glamour faded after a while, though I wouldn't trade the experience for the world, and of course I keep up with the girls. I ended up quitting when I was thirty and becoming a flight attendant. Rick and I met on a flight to Hong Kong. It was lust at first sight. Ever heard of the mile-high club? We conceived our first child in an airplane lavatory." There was a long silence. Ben cleared his throat. This was the most fun she'd had in a month.

"Gotcha," she said finally. "I worked in public relations. I can't do a high kick to save my life, and I've never even been to Hong Kong."

Pete and Tad screamed with laughter.

"You had me going!" Gina said.

Ben shook his head in admiration. "You could make a

living as an actress."

Eve twinkled in the light of their attention. "Oh, now. Do I really seem like the mile-high type?"

"Never mind a Rockette," Pete said.

Dinner was served by a maid who wore a black dress and frilly white apron. Eve thought the costume was Ben and Helene's idea of a joke; she'd never seen anything like it in real life. Rick sat next to Helene, who ignored him in favor of Pete. At the other end of the table, Ben held forth about politics. Eve worried that Rick wasn't having a good time, but Ben was his friend and he'd wanted to come, so it was on him if he wasn't having fun. She was happy enough eating grilled tuna and chocolate mousse in a little porcelain cup while exchanging wry remarks with Timothy, who was as nice as Pete was not. Tad talked about himself. Gina flirted with Ben. Pete and Helene were as thick as thieves.

When the mousse cups were cleared and the coffee finished, Helene produced a joint. "I got this from an economics major at U Conn," she said as she lit up. "Lovely boy. Making money hand over fist. He's got everything you could want: cocaine, pills, whatever."

She took a toke and passed the joint to Rick. He looked at it as if he'd never seen such a thing, then took a little puff. When it came around to Eve, she almost said no. She hadn't smoked pot in decades.

"Oh well, okay," she said. She took the joint. The smoke rasped her throat. She held it in her lungs for a few seconds and coughed as she exhaled.

Timothy applauded her. "That's the way, Rockette!"

"I don't know what possessed me to say that," Eve said. "My kids love the Rockettes. We always go to the *Christmas Spectacular*. They dress up like toy soldiers, it's cute."

"Your kids dress up as toy soldiers?" Gina said. She took

a toke and waved the smoke away from her face.

"No, the Rockettes do," Eve said.

"Oh God, you're not going to talk about your children, are you?" Pete said.

"She's not," Gina said. "I asked a question. People do have kids, Pete. They refer to them sometimes in conversation."

"Sadly," Pete said. "'Never work with children or animals.' Do you know who said that?"

"W. C. Fields," Eve said. All of a sudden she was as stoned as she'd ever been. Pete's head appeared to shrink. She looked at Helene, who was taking a second toke. "What's in that stuff?"

"Marijuana," Helene said.

"That's right, W. C. Fields!" Pete said. "You should go on *Jeopardy!*"

"I knew someone who was on *Jeopardy!*" Gina said. "A girl I went to college with. The funny thing is, she didn't even seem that smart."

"Let's go into the living room," Helene said. She got up and stumbled on the flagstones. "Watch out, everyone!" She giggled.

The light in the living room was rosy and mellow. Eve sat down in a deep, snowy couch and lit a cigarette.

"Feel free," Helene said. "Go right ahead."

"Can I bum one?" Gina said. Eve handed her the pack. "To tell you the truth, I can see you as a Rockette. Those long legs of yours."

"Dance, Rockette!" Pete said. "Show us a high kick!"

"You know what kind of dancing I love?" Eve said. "Swing dancing."

"Oh, I love swing too!" Timothy said. Eve squinted at him. His voice echoed as if from a cave. "Ben, find something on Spotify we can dance to."

Ben lumbered out of the room. In a minute, "Boogie

Woogie Bugle Boy" came through invisible speakers. Eve snapped her fingers in time to the music. She was a good dancer, but Rick would never oblige her, and perhaps he was right not to: he danced with a bumbling lack of focus that made him impossible to follow. He sat on the opposite couch drinking a snifter of something tawny. She looked at him. *Home soon,* he mouthed. Or maybe he said it aloud.

"Come on!" Timothy said and pulled her up off the couch. He took her into his arms with surprising strength and assurance, leading her over Helene's carpet. It had been years since she'd danced even a foxtrot; it took her a moment to catch the rhythm and move as one with Timothy. She felt the flexibility of youth return to her limbs as she ducked under his arm and twirled out again. He pulled her to him and they rocked vigorously back and forth.

"He's in the army now," he sang. "Ta dah, ta dah, ta dah."

"I think I better stop," Eve said after a few minutes. "I'm dizzy from all this twirling."

"Helene!" Timothy called. "Take Eve's place."

"I don't know how," Helene said.

"I do," Gina said. She got up and joined him. Eve was released.

"Bathroom?" she said to Helene.

"Through there, first door on your left."

She sat on the toilet, and with her elbows on her thighs she rested her head in her hands. If she closed her eyes, the world stopped whirling. Most "good times" weren't particularly fun, she decided: fun was for children and simpletons. After a while she exchanged the toilet for the floor and lay on the cool tiles like a starfish. The ceiling was painted with vines and fronds and colorful birds, a genteel Connecticut jungle, as if Helene and Ben expected people to lie on the floor all the time and wanted to give them something to look at. The smell of gardenias or jasmine came from a scented candle. She thought she could stay here all night.

There was a knock on the door. Helene peeked in.

"I thought you looked green around the gills," she said. She extended her hand and helped Eve up. "I guess the pot disagreed with you. And you drank an awful lot of wine."

"Oh, I'm sorry," Eve said. "I didn't mean to."

"Nobody does," Helene said. "Gladys has a habit of topping off people's glasses, so you never know how much you've had. I've told her not to time and again. She's as dumb as a box of hammers."

"She looked pretty silly in that maid's costume," Eve said.

"I know, right?" Helene said. "Ben insisted. He thinks it's classy." She laughed shortly. "He doesn't have the first idea what classy is."

They went out to the living room. Eve gingerly sat down. Helene brought her a glass of water. Pete and Timothy were slow dancing to "April in Paris" like teenagers in love.

"Where is Rick?" Eve said. No one answered. She went upstairs and looked in all the guest rooms, three of them, empty and spotless. Lingering in the vast master bathroom, she examined Helene's army of face creams and potions, dabbed perfume on the insides of her wrists. The bathtub was reached by two marble steps; the shower was the kind that shot jets of water from the walls. She checked out the contents of the medicine cabinet: Klonopin, Vicodin, codeine; Sensodyne, Advil, Certain Dri. She took a Klonopin, put it back, and swallowed two Advil instead.

"Does anyone know where Rick went?" she said when she came back downstairs.

"Home, probably," Tad said. He sat next to Helene, smoking another joint. "I saw him go out of the room with a pretty glum look on his face."

Eve went to the front hall and looked through the screen door. Their car was still in the driveway. She walked out to see if Rick was sitting inside it, which he might have been if he was feeling sulky enough. Cupping her mouth with her hands, she called his name. Nothing. The pulsing scream of late summer crickets and the fainter sound of "April in Paris."

Lit only by the moon, the steps were rickety and steep. Eve hung on to the single railing with both hands and crept down to the river. She knew Rick was down there, she could feel it, though he didn't answer when she called. She was afraid he'd fallen and was lying unconscious on the beach or had drowned in the placid water. She reached the dock and walked out to where Ben's boat was tied up at the end. It was a speedboat, sleek as Ben's Ferrari. Rick was sitting behind the wheel.

"Jesus, Rick. I nearly broke my neck on those stairs. What are you doing?"

"I was thinking about going for a ride," he said. He held up a tiny replica of a buoy with a key dangling from one end. "I found it on a hook inside the front door."

"Get out of there and let's go home."

"Join me." He patted the seat beside him.

"Just for a minute," she said. She took off her sandals and climbed over the side of the boat. Rick's face in the moonlight was dead white. "I guess you weren't having fun."

"No, but you were. 'Dance, Rockette!'" he said in a fair imitation of Pete's nasal voice.

"I embarrassed you, is that it?"

"Yes. No."

"Which?"

"I want this," he said.

"This boat?"

"This boat, this house, this everything. I'll never have anything like it. There's no way in the world."

Eve was silent. Water lapped against the boat's hull. A village winked on the opposite shore. Rick sighed.

"I loved high school. You know that; I've told you about

it. Ben is right, I was cool. I was the goddamn prom king, the captain of the football team. I was the cliché."

"You enjoyed yourself," Eve said. "Not everybody can say that about high school."

"I think those years were the best of my life."

"You don't love these years?" she said. "Being married to me, raising our kids?"

"I like these years fine," he said.

"But they're not what you imagined for yourself."

He shrugged. "Don't most people imagine something better for themselves than what they end up getting?"

"Not me," Eve said. "I love you; I love my children. I have enough, and I feel lucky." It was true, more or less. She was mostly content. She started to get up. Rick could fuck off.

"Wait." He grabbed her arm. "Go for a ride with me."

"You can't run off with Ben's boat."

"Why can't I? I'll return it. He's too stoned to notice."

She sat down again. She was still pretty stoned herself. She put her fingers to the outer edges of her eyes and felt two nests of deeply etched lines. Rick was still handsome, not a strand of gray in his hair, the prom king forevermore. "Do you think Helene is beautiful? Do you want her as well?"

"I don't want her," Rick said.

He untied the line and turned the key in the ignition. Slowly, he reversed the boat until it was clear of the dock. As he gunned the motor and the engine roared, Eve felt a ghost of a thrill. The river ahead was undisturbed, a sheet of black glass to be shattered.

NEXT OF KIN

It was a middle-of-the-night sort of phone call that came on a Saturday afternoon, a New York City police officer asking if I knew a man named Basil Farley. I'd known him at one time, I said, but I didn't know him anymore. I hadn't seen him in ages. Basil had been my mother's boyfriend—her "beau," as she called him—during the last years of her life.

"He was clipped by a cab on Second Avenue this morning," the officer said. "It looked like he'd be fine except for a broken leg, but then he had a heart attack at the hospital. I'm sorry."

"You mean he's dead?" I said.

"I'm afraid so."

"But why are you calling me about it?"

"He listed you as his next of kin."

"I'm not, though. He has a daughter." I struggled to remember her name.

"He's at Lenox Hill Hospital," the officer said and gave me a number to call. I wrote it down on a clothing catalog, scrawled across a photo of an ecru alpaca wrap. "They can suggest a funeral home if you don't have one in mind."

"A funeral home? But I'm not responsible for him." He had hung up.

I'd been on my way out to meet a friend for lunch, a rare book dealer named Sid whom I was actively wooing despite his obvious lack of interest. We were both in our early forties, and neither of us had been married, which made me a spinster and him a catch. I called him and told him what had happened. He asked if he could help. That was how he was. *You could fall madly in love with me,* I thought. I very nearly said it.

"What would happen if I just left him there?" I said.

"They might hound you about him," he said.

"Do you think I'll have to give him a funeral?" I didn't have the money for even a pine box. My freelance job scouting celebrity interviews for a gossip magazine was barely enough to keep me afloat. "It's just so weird that he had my number. What am I going to do?"

"A step at a time," Sid said. "Call the hospital first."

The number I called was answered by a woman's brusque voice. I explained myself and was told that I had to come to the hospital to retrieve Basil's possessions.

"I'd rather not," I said. "Can't you just give them away?"

"There's a gold watch and a leather wallet with three hundred twenty dollars in it," she said. "You got seventy-two hours to collect the body."

"What happens after seventy-two hours?"

"State takes it," she said. "Body goes to science."

"Well, that's a good cause," I said.

"I wouldn't want it for my father," she said.

"He's not my father."

"Wouldn't want it for anyone," she said. "Room 1B06, use the east side entrance, elevator to the first basement. I'm here until five."

The hospital wasn't far, so I walked there. It was the first really beautiful day of spring after weeks of chilly rain, and the pear trees were snowing blossoms. I lived on East Sixty-Ninth Street in a studio apartment that I had rigged up with a curtain so it looked like two rooms. At one time I had owned a one-bedroom in the West Village, but the morning talk show for which I'd worked as a producer was canceled a few years back, and I ended up having to find somewhere less expensive to live. My forty-two-year-old life closely resembled what my life had looked like at twenty-five, when I lived in a shoebox apartment and worked a job I considered a waste of my talent and time.

The brusque woman at the hospital was as small as her voice was large. Her thick blond hair was teased into a helmet-shaped bouffant and held fast to her head by a wide, red barrette. I wondered where someone so tiny bought their clothes. In the children's department, I guessed. There was nothing childish about her, though; she had an unusually dignified air considering she was only about four feet tall. She slid off her desk chair and went to a double row of gray metal lockers stacked on top of each other.

"Help me with this," she said, pointing to an upper locker. I went over and opened it. There was a clear plastic bag as big as a bed pillow that held a tweed jacket and a pair of gray flannel pants, a wallet, a set of keys, and a handful of loose change. The watch was a Rolex.

"This is his stuff?" I said.

"You tell me," she said. She went back to her desk and climbed onto her chair. "You have to verify that everything is there."

"I wouldn't know," I said. "I haven't seen him in years."

"Your own father, what a tragedy," she said, pushing a form across the desk.

"He's not—" I began but decided not to bother.

In the hospital lobby, I sat on a bench and fished Basil's wallet from the bottom of the bag. I pocketed the cash and extracted his driver's license from behind a chunk of credit cards. On the license was his address. I took my phone from my purse and called Sid.

"Will you come with me to Basil's apartment?"

"Sure," he said. "I'll meet you there."

I strapped the Rolex loosely around my wrist. I would need to have it adjusted. "Guess what?" I said. "The woman who gave me his stuff was a midget."

"Wow, no kidding. You never see midgets anymore. Why is that, I wonder?" We were silent for a moment, considering the question. "Or dwarves either," he said.

I didn't want to make a thing out of Basil being dead until I could find someone to take responsibility for his body, so I told the doorman at Basil's building on Fifth Avenue that I was Basil's visiting niece. I was wearing leggings and a tattered hoodie, but Sid looked respectable in a blue cashmere sweater and jeans that he had ironed so many times they had pale creases down their legs. There were nerdy things about Sid I ignored—who cared that he wore a white undershirt that showed beneath his collar, or laughed in a dry "hee-hee-hee" way, like a dastardly cartoon character? He was sweet and almost handsome in a Clark Kent–ish manner, shorter than I was, but that was okay. I wondered what he thought of me more than I should have. I wasn't so fabulous either.

After some confusion with the locks and keys, we let ourselves into Basil's apartment. On a round table in the foyer sat a delicious smelling arrangement of white peonies and lilac. The flowers were fresh, perhaps delivered that morning. He'd expected to come home, like everyone did.

We went into the living room. It was high-ceilinged, with three big windows facing the park. There was a conglomeration of upholstered furniture covered in matching green-and-white chintz, and side tables with knickknacks displayed on their polished surfaces, china figurines and miniature paintings, a carved ivory fan, a purple crystal on a stand. I picked up a netsuke of a sleeping dog I admired and slipped it into my pocket.

"What was he like?" Sid said. He was perusing the

books in a gigantic built-in bookcase. He took out a book. "Leatherbound. Nice."

"He was short and chubby. And bald," I said.

"No, I meant, what kind of person was he?"

I thought about it. A rich person, obviously. My mother, who'd had very little money herself, had made a point of dating rich men. "Very polite. Old fashioned. He always stood up when I came into the room. I didn't see him very often, but we always got along." My mother hadn't been in love with him, or with any of her other boyfriends either. Not for the first time, I wondered if she'd ever been in love.

"It must have been hell growing up with a name like Basil."

"*Bah*sil," I drawled. "It suited him, though."

I went back out to the foyer and down a short hall that led to Basil's bedroom. A queen-size bed was flanked by matching nightstands that held stacks of hardcover novels and biographies. I picked one up: *The Audacity of Hope* by Barack Obama, dog-eared in several places. I wouldn't have taken him for a Democrat. Certainly my mother hadn't been one. The nightstands' shallow drawers offered not much more than medication bottles, nail clippers and a file, and a white, palm-sized bible. In between the pages of the bible was a studio photograph of Basil as a young man with a curly-haired little girl perched on his knee. I remembered his daughter's name: Arabella. I'd never met her, but Basil once said I should, because she and I were about the same age.

"I have a very strong feeling the daughter is dead," I shouted to Sid as I sat down on the bed. He was wandering around somewhere. When he came in, I showed him the bible and the photograph. "Because why else wouldn't he have given her name as next of kin?"

"Uh oh," Sid said. "Well, he must have a lawyer. Everyone has a lawyer."

"I don't." I would list Sid as my next of kin, I thought,

and make him responsible for my body. "Did you see a den or an office?"

He shook his head. "There's a little desk in the living room, but it looks like he only used it to store tax returns and bank statements. I looked for a will, but I didn't find one. Otherwise, there's only this room and a dining room off the kitchen. Considering his age, he didn't have much stuff. My parents have so much worthless junk in their house you can barely get through the door."

I wondered, if Basil's daughter was dead, had he made me a beneficiary of his will? I couldn't think why he would have. Already, I was spending the imaginary money and planning to move into his apartment. I looked around: I would paint the bedroom periwinkle blue and replace the queen bed with a king.

"I need to find his address book," I said. There hadn't been a cell phone in the bag with his effects, but there was an ancient touch-tone phone by the bed. *Old people*, I thought impatiently. My mother had died without ever using an ATM; she'd written checks at the bank when she needed cash, standing in line for the teller. She'd had a fat leather address book full of disconnected old numbers and outdated addresses, but she could always find who she was looking for. Basil had to have had something like that. Eventually I would scare up a friend or a relative.

His chest of drawers held neatly folded boxer shorts and shirts, argyle socks rolled into balls; his closet, hung with a surprising number of trousers and sport jackets, smelled like mothballs and lime aftershave. There were shoes fitted with wooden shoe trees and sweaters stacked on the shelves. Everything was just so. If I were to die that minute, Sid would find a half-eaten bag of Doritos in my unmade bed and yesterday's underpants on the bathroom floor.

I gazed out the window while I tried to think where else an address book would be. The sun streamed low and golden through the trees in the park, painting half the street. It was closing in on cocktail hour. "I wonder if he has anything to drink."

"We can't drink his liquor," Sid said in a scandalized voice.

"Of course we can," I said. Sid grinned at me as if I were a mischievous child. I hadn't meant to come off as mischievous; I was just dying for a glass of wine.

On a counter in the kitchen there was a wrought iron wine rack that held a few bottles of Bordeaux; a large blue bottle of Bombay gin sat nearby on a brass-handled wooden tray. I uncorked a Bordeaux and found a wineglass. The kitchen was gloomy with only a single window that looked out on a brick wall. The yellow linoleum floor was scratched and worn, and the appliances looked as if they'd been bought in the past century. I looked in the fridge. Half a lemon, an unopened bottle of tonic, and two bottles of what appeared to be expensive champagne. The Formica-and-chrome table and matching chairs were so old they were back in fashion.

"Wine?" I said to Sid as I took down another glass.

He was scrabbling around in a drawer, taking out items and dropping them back in. He pulled out a creased paper menu and let it flutter to the floor. "Gross, there are mouse droppings in here!" he said and rushed to the sink to wash his hands.

I picked up the menu. "I remember this restaurant. It's around the corner. Basil used to take my mother there all the time." Basil had circled several dishes on the menu in pencil. "He must have ordered his meals from here. How sad." I imagined him sitting at the table all by himself dining on *boeuf en croûte* and floating island and drinking a glass of champagne. There was a little TV on the counter opposite the table. He had probably watched it while he was eating.

"Drawer number *two*," Sid said. "Oh! Silver flatware." He held a fork up to the overhead light. "Kirk Stieff Repousse.

Gorgeous."

I watched him through my wineglass. I wished he would look at me the way he was looking at that fork. "Hey, I'm starving," I said. "Let's order something to eat."

"I don't know, it feels weird to hang around here. Let's go get sushi or something."

"But look, they have Dover sole!" I said. We both loved Dover sole.

He blinked at the menu. "Whoa, for thirty dollars.

"Live a little," I said. I picked up the receiver of a wall-mounted phone—an old touch-tone like the one in the bedroom—and dialed the number of the restaurant. Taped to the wall beside the phone was an index card printed with phone numbers for the front desk in the lobby, a dry cleaner, a grocery store, a pharmacy, and someone named Mrs. Gomez. At the bottom of the list "Arabella" was written above a phone number with an unfamiliar area code. Both the name and the number had lines drawn through them, scratched out but still legible, which made me wonder if she was estranged from Basil rather than dead. I could have called the number immediately and found out which, but I wasn't in the mood just then to give or hear unhappy news.

I set the dining room table with an embroidered white cloth and two gold-rimmed plates that I found in a glass-fronted sideboard. If Basil had given dinner parties, he hadn't given one in a long time, because the cloth smelled musty and the plates were sticky with dust, requiring a wash. When I lived in the Village, I'd given a lot of parties. I missed the excitement of preparing for guests, the buzz of a packed dinner table. Being invited to a party wasn't nearly as fun as giving one of my own, but I never had people over to my place on Sixty-Ninth. It was too small to entertain in, and, frankly embarrassing: I didn't need to view my diminished life through anyone else's eyes.

Sid was at the living room bookcase again, a proverbial bee to honey. "I wonder if I can buy some of these books from Basil's estate," he said as I walked in. I filled his empty glass from a fresh bottle of wine. He showed me a book. "*House of Mirth*, first edition."

"Just take it," I said.

He replaced the book. "Grave robber," he said. "You can't just take a dead person's things."

"Yes, you can. When my aunt died, I took all her jewelry."

"Because she was your aunt," Sid said. "You had a relationship."

"I had somewhat of a relationship with Basil a while ago. And, hello, I'm his next of kin." I took the book from the shelf again. "Here, I'm giving it to you as a present." He looked at the empty slot in the bookcase, then back at the book. Clearly he wanted to have it. The doorbell rang. "Food's here!" I said and thrust it into his hands.

I arranged the sole and vegetables on our plates and lit four candles in a silver candelabra. The dining room had only an overhead light that I was certain made me look haggard, so I turned it off and we ate in a pool of candlelight that was either spooky or romantic. I poured champagne into a pair of crystal flutes.

"To Basil," I said, raising my glass.

"Poor guy," Sid said.

"Well, if you have to go, I think a heart attack is a pretty good way." My mother had died a long and agonizing death from esophageal cancer.

"But dying alone?" Sid said. "I wouldn't want that."

Me either, I thought, but unless Sid or some other man stepped up, dying alone was where I was headed. Back in the days when my life made sense, I'd had a boyfriend I'd expect-ed to eventually marry until he moved to Los Angeles for a job. Stupidly, I hadn't gone with him because of *my* job (soon to be nonexistent) and because I didn't want to be the kind of woman who gave things up for a man. Quite the feminist I was. Thinking about it made me grimace.

"What's wrong?" Sid said. "You okay?" His forehead was creased with concern.

God, how I loved his thoughtfulness. "Not a thing!" I said. "What could be wrong?"

"Oh, I don't know. We're sitting in a dead man's dining room, which in theory could be depressing."

"Yet in actuality it's very pleasant," I said. If he disagreed, I couldn't tell.

"You know, I bet the doorman would know the names of a few of Basil's friends," he said. "Doormen are in on everything. What do you think?"

For a moment I didn't know what to say. Of course he was right. "It's an idea," I said. "But I already told him I'm Basil's niece. I'd have to admit I was lying."

"He won't care," Sid said. He took a bite of his sole. "Delicious."

"Isn't it? My mother loved Dover sole, too." This also was a lie; she'd hated fish, but I knew that my lack of family pulled heavily at Sid's heart strings. He reached over and patted the table an inch from my hand, as if he'd been going for the hand and missed.

I poured the last two inches of the champagne into our glasses and went to open the second bottle. When I came back, Sid was eating buttered asparagus with his fingers, which if not exactly sexy made me think about sex. I kicked off my sneakers, sat down, and felt for his leg with my foot. I found his thigh and scooted down in my chair until my toe touched what I hoped was his crotch.

"Oh," he said, looking down at his lap. "What are you up to?"

"Taking things in hand," I said. "Or rather, in foot." He continued to look at his crotch as if shocked to find it there.

I slid off my chair and ducked under the tablecloth, plunging into darkness so black I was momentarily unmoored. On my hands and knees, I crawled to him and felt for the zipper of his pants. His penis was limp but grew hard when I put it in my mouth. Giving a blowjob was a rarity for me, it just wasn't my forte, but what I lacked in technique I made up for in determination. When he was good and hard and breathing heavily, I crawled back out from under the table. I took his hand.

"Come on," I said, leading him toward Basil's bedroom. He looked ridiculous with a massive hard-on poking out of his fly.

"I don't think . . . ," he said.

"*Don't* think," I said.

Basil's bedroom was dark. I went to turn on a lamp.

"No," Sid said. "Leave it off."

I fell onto the bed and pulled him on top of me. We kissed aggressively for a while, our tongues wrestling with each other, then I peeled off my leggings and unbuckled his belt. I felt for his penis. It was limp again.

"What can I do to remedy this?" I said. "Tell me what you like."

There was a long moment when we stared at each other's indistinct faces, pale ovals in the dark. "Guys," he said finally.

"Guys?" I said.

"I like men. I'm gay."

I sat up and snapped on the bedside light. Basil's bedroom sprang to life. "Gay?" I said loudly. I pulled up my leggings and readjusted my hoodie. Basil's netsuke fell out of my pocket and rolled off the bed onto the floor. "Jesus, Sid, you should have told me."

"I thought it was obvious!" he said as he pulled himself together. "I mean, come on. You must have known on some level."

Wishful thinking, I thought. Sure, he wasn't the manliest

of men, but I hadn't considered him particularly effeminate either. I'd thought he was being polite when he never
mentioned ex-girlfriends, but he hadn't told me about any
boyfriends either, so I didn't think I'd been that dense. I had
been working on him for more than three months, ever since
we met at a mutual friend's party.

"What a waste of time," I said.

"Wow, thanks. I thought we've been having a lot of fun
together, but I guess not."

"No, we were," I said. "We do. But I wanted you to be in
love with me."

He drew back. "Are you in love with me?"

I paused. "Okay, good point. But I could potentially be.
I like you better than any guy I've known."

"I like you better than anyone too. We think the same
things are funny, we always have a lot to talk about. We enjoy
each other's company! Don't you know how unusual it is to
make a new friend at our age?"

"Our age. Right." I flopped back on the bed and stared
at the ceiling. Basil's sheets smelled like they needed to be
washed, body odor mixed with the tang of his cologne. The
last time I'd seen him was at the hospital when my mother
was days from death. I must have given him my phone number then. I was surprised to feel tears slide down the sides of
my face. I hadn't known I was crying. "Sid?" I said. "Will you
be my next of kin?"

"I'd like nothing better," he said. He lay down next to me
and put his arm over my waist. We fell asleep like that. Like
lovers.

ACKNOWLEDGMENTS

I wrote many of these stories during the first year of the pandemic when I, like everyone, was terrified. How fortunate I was to be able to write through those sad days, and in writing to forget reality. I thank the kind angel who gave me that gift, and who continues to perch on my shoulder.

LOUISE MARBURG

My appreciation for these generous friends cannot be overstated: Jill McCorkle critiqued every story and arranged them in their present order; she read my tarot cards and cheered me on during lockdown and beyond. A story isn't finished until the brilliant and discerning Katrina Denza signs off on it. Kris Faatz is my editor extraordinaire. April Nauman, I cherish your keen eye and our endless laughs. When I grow up, I want to be as whip smart as Sharon Harrigan, and as full of grace and kindness as Lisa Cupolo. I am blessed to have found my wonderful publicist, Julia Borcherts. My cousin, David Schweizer, is my unfailingly loyal fan. Chris Cander, we are a gang: you keep me afloat every day.

I am grateful for the support of the Virginia Center for the Creative Arts and the Sewanee Writer's Conference.

Keith Lesmeister, thank you for laughing out loud.